## Here's what critics are saying about
### Leslie Langtry's books:

"I laughed so hard I cried on multiple occasions while reading MARSHMALLOW S'MORE MURDER! Girl Scouts, the CIA, and the Yakuza... what could possibly go wrong?"
—Fresh Fiction

"Darkly funny and wildly over the top, this mystery answers the burning question, 'Do assassin skills and Girl Scout merit badges mix...' one truly original and wacky novel!"
—RT BOOK REVIEWS

"Those who like dark humor will enjoy a look into the deadliest female assassin and PTA mom's life."
—Parkersburg News

"Mixing a deadly sense of humor and plenty of sexy sizzle, Leslie Langtry creates a brilliantly original, laughter-rich mix of contemporary romance and suspense in *'Scuse Me While I Kill This Guy.*"
—Chicago Tribune

"The beleaguered soccer mom assassin concept is a winner, and Langtry gets the fun started from page one with a myriad of clever details."
—Publisher's Weekly

D1523213

# BOOKS BY LESLIE LANGTRY

*Merry Wrath Mysteries:*
Merit Badge Murder
Mint Cookie Murder
Scout Camp Murder
(short story in the Killer Beach Reads collection)
Marshmallow S'More Murder
Movie Night Murder
Mud Run Murder
Fishing Badge Murder
(short story in the Pushing Up Daisies collection)
Motto for Murder
Map Skills Murder
Mean Girl Murder
Marriage Vow Murder

*Greatest Hits Mysteries:*
'Scuse Me While I Kill This Guy
Guns Will Keep Us Together
Stand By Your Hitman
I Shot You Babe
Paradise By The Rifle Sights
Snuff the Magic Dragon
My Heroes Have Always Been Hitmen
Have Yourself a Deadly Little Christmas (a holiday short story)

*Aloha Lagoon Mysteries:*
Ukulele Murder
Ukulele Deadly

*Other Works:*
Sex, Lies, & Family Vacations

# MARRIAGE VOW MURDER

### A Merry Wrath Mystery

## USA TODAY BESTSELLING AUTHOR
# Leslie Langtry

# MARRIAGE VOW MURDER

# CHAPTER ONE

———

"What do you mean, there's a body in the front pew?" I asked my best friend and matron of honor. (BTW, that title has nothing to do with prison or knights in shining armor. I checked.)

My wedding was set for tomorrow, December 28. With the rehearsal dinner later tonight, Kelly and I thought we'd get a jump on decorating the church—which meant she was decorating and telling me I was doing it wrong. We'd only been there one hour before she sprung this on me.

Kelly's face had gone a little green, which was odd, considering the fact that she was a nurse. "I think it's the florist."

"The florist is dead?" That didn't seem like good news. "Did he drop off the flowers first?"

Kelly's jaw dropped. "Merry!"

"What? We paid a fortune for those flowers!"

Okay, maybe she had a point and I was being a tad insensitive, but I was running on wedding stress—a stress I found strangely similar to armed-showdown-in-an-Estonian-alley stress or hand-over-the-photos-to-a-dwarf-dressed-as-an-astronaut-with-a-flamethrower-while-standing-on-the-edge-of-a-cliff-in-Peru stress.

My to-do list was ridiculous. I followed Kelly to the front of the church, and there was elderly Lewis Spitz, my florist, lying there, with a knife sticking out of his chest.

"Another murder in my vicinity." With a heavy sigh, I took out my cell.

My fiancé was also the town detective. He was wrapping up a few loose ends at work before the wedding tomorrow. Now he'd have a murder to deal with.

Officer Kevin Dooley, a mouth breather and paste eater I'd known since kindergarten, arrived alone, with his arm elbow deep in a bag of pork rinds.

I looked behind Kevin and asked, "Where's Rex?"

The officer's expression resembled a lobotomized amoeba. "He's not at the station. We've tried to get hold of him. He's missing."

I hadn't heard anything more than grunts from this guy for three years. He finally strung more than one word together, and it was to say my fiancé had gone missing? I pulled out my cell and called Rex. After five rings it went into voicemail.

"He's here somewhere," I said as I turned on a tracking app I'd recently installed on our phones.

And, no, it's not *Find My iPhone* (although that is useful). It's a special CIA app I'd hacked that takes things to a whole new level. It can tell you where someone is, what they're wearing, and what they're eating—an unfortunate addition, as Rex has discovered I like to eat Oreos in the parking lot of one of the local grocery stores.

In this case, however, the app was a bust. There was no signal at all. Nothing indicating Rex's location or even his existence. I called his twin sisters and his parents next. Nobody had seen or heard from him today.

When had I seen him last? Last night when we had pizza at my house—a quiet moment for just the two of us, his dog, and my cats before the chaos to come. I tried calling him once more without luck.

Fortunately, my dress for the rehearsal was hanging in the dressing room. I was still wearing jeans, a sweatshirt, and boots—which would be better for running around in the snow. Why we picked December for a wedding was beyond me.

"Where are you going?" Kelly called out.

"I'll be right back," I shouted over my shoulder as I tore up the aisle.

This had to be some sort of miscommunication. Maybe Rex was working on a surprise for me. I did love a good surprise. So why were my spy-dy senses tingling as I drove to his house a few blocks away?

By the way, everything in Who's There, Iowa, was a few blocks away. In fact, the town motto for decades has been *You can go anywhere in Who's There in five minutes*. Inspiring stuff that never convinced anyone to move or locate their business here.

As for Rex, until I knew more, I was going to keep a lid on my fears. Fears that included the idea that he'd gotten cold feet and run off...or that he'd been held up by some last-minute detail.

Leonard, the Scottish deerhound, greeted me at Rex's house with a confused look and excited tail wag that cleared the coffee table.

"Rex!" I shouted as I ran through the home.

His car was in the garage, but he wasn't. I kept calling his name. There was no answer after a very thorough search that included the cupboard under the sink and the bathroom medicine cabinet. Why? You can never be too sure. Once, in Japan, I found a man living in the bathroom wall. He wasn't a spy but a weirdo with a medicine cabinet fetish. His name was Ted.

I ran across the street to my house as I called his cell for the fifth time. This time, it skipped the rings and went straight to voicemail. Which meant he was either "declining" my calls or his phone was switched off.

The cats looked suspiciously at me as if to say whatever was wrong must be my fault. They didn't even help me look, which made me wonder if they were covering for him. They weren't. Rex wasn't at my house either.

I called Kelly, but she told me that Rex hadn't checked in or shown up. In fact, his sisters, Randi and Ronni, and his parents were there and worried.

"Get back here soon!" Kelly whispered into the phone. "Randi is setting up a dead otter nativity! Between that and the dead body in the first pew, Pastor Brown is not happy!"

Randi and her twin sister, Ronni, were taxidermists here in town. Since I'd met them last spring, I'd been the doubtful recipient of many dead animals in bizarre dioramas. The two short, plump women created anthropomorphic taxidermy—animals posed like humans, doing human things. It was disturbing at first, but over the last several months I'd become numb to the absurdity of it all. Pastor Brown, on the other hand, would be new to this.

"Have Mom handle it," I told her. "I've got to find Rex."

She agreed and hung up before I could respond. My mother, Judith Czrygy, was a senator's wife and was the only one who could say no to the twins in a way that seemed like an overwhelmingly enthusiastic "yes."

For the next twenty minutes, I drove past every parking lot, business, and home in Who's There, Iowa. I checked every store and restaurant we'd ever been too. Kelly texted that no one at the hospital had seen him. My fiancé had simply disappeared.

Where was he? Now the fears started creeping into my head. Rex wasn't the type to get cold feet and run off. I knew that, and yet it shot to the top of my anxiety list. No, he wouldn't do that. Rex was a responsible adult. If he'd wanted to call it off, he wouldn't have waited until the day before. We would have discussed it a while ago. My fiancé was thoughtful, smart, and mature, and he didn't hide from his concerns.

Which meant he was either lost or abducted. And since Who's There is a small town of maybe eight thousand people, getting lost wasn't an option. Granted, he could've gotten lost in the maze of gravel roads and cornfields that surrounded us in every direction. One time, when I was in high school and detassling corn for the summer, they bussed in some kids from Des Moines. In spite of just having to walk from one end to the other of a row of corn, they got lost and were missing for five hours. We found them in the next county in an unfortunate town called Pig Belly, at the also unfortunately named Tastee Dog. They were dazed and had no idea where they were but had filled up on soft-serve ice cream and corn dogs instead of calling anyone.

Which left one alternative. Rex had been kidnapped or worse. Most small-town cops didn't just disappear. But this police detective had a problem…me.

I had enemies. Up until three years ago, I'd been a spy— a field agent with the CIA. I'd infiltrated drug cartels in Cartagena, spied on the Yakuza in Tokyo, and fought off the FSB in a dark alley in Moscow. So, when the vice president "accidentally" outed me to get back at my dad, a powerful player in the Senate, I changed my name from Fionnaghuala Merrygold Wrath Czrygy to Merry Wrath and moved back to my hometown in Iowa to hide out until I knew what I wanted to do with my life.

Most of the people I'd spied on were in prison or dead now. But it was possible that someone had found out who and where I was…and wanted revenge. Bile rose in my throat as I broke out in a sweat. Was that what happened?

I shook my head to clear it. *Get ahold of yourself, Wrath!* This wasn't an international conspiracy! Rex always said that most abductions were by someone the victim knew (and then there were always aliens). But who would that be? And then it occurred to me.

I had one more place I could check. And it was the last place I wanted to go.

\* \* \*

"Where is he?" I demanded as I stormed into the office in the strip mall.

Riley looked up from his computer. "Where's who?"

I folded my arms over my chest and narrowed my eyes. "Rex. Where is he?"

My former CIA handler grinned smugly. "You don't know where your intended is? Aren't you getting married tomorrow?"

"What did you do with Rex?" I asked in clipped tones so he'd know I meant business.

He held up his hands defensively. All smartassery gone. "What are you talking about?"

My spy-dar told me he was genuinely confused. Riley Andrews was telling the truth. I slumped into a chair and told him everything, from the body in the pew to my search. He listened and even had the grace to look concerned. Riley had been jockeying for my affections over the past three years. When he retired to open a private investigation firm in my hometown, I'd decided to avoid him like a Russian figure skater with leprosy and a spitting problem.

He'd even offered me a job.

I'd turned him down.

"I have no idea where he is, Merry." Riley held up his hands defensively. "I swear."

Riley seemed genuine. His blue eyes were wrinkled with concern as he ran his hands through his wavy blond hair. He was so different from Rex. Where Riley messed with my head, Rex respected me. While Riley was a womanizer, Rex was a one-woman man. The two men couldn't be more different.

I threw my hands up. "Then where is he?"

"Are you sure he's missing?" my former partner asked. "Maybe he told you he was running to Des Moines for something and you forgot?"

I thought about getting indignant, but Riley had a point. In my retirement, I'd become forgetful at times. Had Rex said something about an errand today? I ran through our conversation last night but came up empty, mostly because we'd been talking about my favorite subject—junk food.

"He left his car in his garage," I said. "And he doesn't have a squad car. Which means he didn't go to Des Moines."

"I don't think the police will consider him missing until he's gone twenty-four hours," Riley quipped.

"Did you read that in the private investigator's playbook?" I snapped.

"No," he said, ignoring my tone. "But I did work for the FBI. Remember?"

By now my head was splitting. "I'd better get back to the church." I got to my feet. "But if you know something and aren't telling me, I'll disembowel you with a drinking straw. You know what I mean. Remember Tashkent?" With one more threatening glance, I rushed out of his place and got back into my car.

By the time I walked back into the church, there was a sea of worried faces on our family and friends. Well, except for his sister, Ronni. But then, she always looked angry. Rex's parents were huddled with the twins, Randi and Ronni, talking softly. Did they know something? That seemed unlikely. As much as Ronni despised me, the others seemed to really like me.

Oh, crap. In my insane rush through town, I'd forgotten about Lewis Spitz. Considering the dead florist in the first pew being examined by the coroner who was also my bridesmaid, it was difficult to say what upset folks more. I nodded at Dr. Soo Jin Body, who returned the nod and went back to work.

There was another possibility for Rex's disappearance…

"Kevin," I demanded of the policeman who was almost asleep in a back pew. "Go arrest Juliette Dowd for kidnapping!"

He got to his feet and was about to walk out the door when Kelly stopped him. Hey, I was impressed he'd listened to me. Too bad my best friend wouldn't let him slap the cuffs on Rex's childhood sweetheart—an overly obsessive Girl Scout employee who raged at me on a regular basis.

"I don't think Miss Dowd kidnapped Rex." Kelly shook her head. "There has to be a reasonable explanation."

"Detective Ferguson is missing?" Soo Jin was standing next to me.

We turned to watch as the body of my florist was being carried out on a stretcher by two paramedics.

"Yes," I said, my eyes on the dead man. "Have you heard from him?"

The coroner shook her head slowly. She was incredibly beautiful doing it, with her large sad eyes and silky black bob. The woman could ugly cry and it would be the loveliest thing mankind had ever seen. She was a friend after a rough probationary period, but I still felt a little insecure around someone who was so beautiful that it hurt to look at her.

Officer Dooley stood there, looking around as if he knew he was supposed to do something but had no idea what. What would he do without Rex? The man couldn't tie his shoes without direction. For a nanosecond, I felt a tiny bit of pity for the Neanderthal.

Dr. Body sighed. "I'll accompany Mr. Spitz to the morgue, and then I'll be back for the rehearsal."

Kevin nodded silently and then spotted a plate of cookies that Kelly had brought for us to snack on. They were gone in seconds.

Riley strode through the door, looking worried. Which was a surprise since he'd been barred from the festivities. I thought having a former flame at my wedding would be a tad indiscreet.

I began issuing commands. "Call in satellite imagery. I need visuals of all routes in and out of town."

We'd likely find nothing because there was no CCTV in the US. I'd seen a documentary on it recently, but no amount of arguing could convince Rex that we needed it here in town. In fact, he'd suggested that it would be more prudent to fit me with body cams—considering all the corpses that showed up around me on a regular basis.

"Surely you don't think he did a runner," Riley protested.

I shook my head. "No. But we have a dead florist. Rex's disappearance is suspicious."

I looked over at Kevin, who had managed to get hopelessly tangled up in a pew bow. It was the night before my wedding day, and my groom was missing. This was definitely going to throw a damper on the rehearsal dinner.

I turned to Riley and said something I never thought I'd say to him.

"I think I need your help."

# CHAPTER TWO

———

A few hours later, as the daylight began to fade, there was a packed church full of concerned people, but no Rex. Soo Jin had the presence of mind to call Sheriff Carnack, and the large, amiable man was walking around, interviewing folks about the murder of Lewis Spitz—something I kept forgetting about.

His two deputies were out looking for the man I was supposed to marry. I liked the sheriff and had far more faith in him than in Officer Kevin Dooley.

Were these two things related? Could Rex be tied to the dead man somehow? Was that worth mentioning to the sheriff? It looked like he had his hands full with the murder and the missing detective. I felt a little sorry for him. Even though his office was in Who's There, most of his work took him to other parts of the county.

You might think that in a county made up entirely of small towns that there wasn't much for law enforcement to do. And you'd be wrong. Just last week, there'd been the kidnapping of a prized cow (it wasn't stolen—it had just wandered off), the theft of a tractor (taken on a joyride by teenagers), and a prison break at a nursing home, where five geriatric men with dementia had escaped, looking in the outskirts of town for a bordello that had ceased to exist in 1929. There's never a dull moment in rural Iowa.

A squeal erupted from the front of the church, and I was soon engulfed in a wave of ten little girls. My Girl Scout troop, which was also the world's largest flower girl contingent, surrounded me with giggles and questions about the rehearsal. They had no idea what was going on.

I held up the silent sign, and they quieted down. Now that I had their attention, I had no idea what to tell them. Kelly, spotting the look on my face, hurried over.

"Why don't you go get something to eat?" She nudged me in the elbow. "I'll talk to the girls."

I wasn't hungry, but since I didn't want to have to explain, one more time, that Rex was missing, I did what she said. Because of Kevin, the platter of cookies was empty, but my mother handed me a package of Oreos, and I began to munch.

"I'm sure he's around here somewhere." Mom put her arm around me.

My dad, Senator Michael Czrygy, put his arm around me, and we stood there in a three-way hug for a few moments. As soothing as it was, it didn't really help.

"It's been *hours*, Mom," I complained. "He was supposed to be here half an hour ago to get ready for the rehearsal. Where is he?"

My mother, who'd once brokered a peace deal between Israel and Iran over a black forest cake at Senator John McCain's Porkstravaganza Barbecue, had nothing to say. That was a bad omen.

"Mrs. Wrath!" Betty screeched as she, Lauren, Inez, and Hannah joined me. "We just heard!"

For years my troop has labored under the delusion that if you're over twenty, you're a Mrs. No matter how much I explained that I was really a Ms., the girls insisted on calling me Mrs. To be honest—they'd soon be right, once I found Rex.

"Do you think the Russians got him?" Lauren asked.

Inez nodded. "Or the mafia?"

"Don't be ridiculous!" Betty shut them down. "It's obvious he's been kidnapped by Basque Separatists!"

I wish! Frankly, Basque Separatists were far easier to handle than not knowing what was going on.

"Maybe," Caterina said, "he's tracking a serial killer who stole his cell phone, through the wilderness! He has no way to contact Mrs. Wrath—and he has to capture the killer at any cost!"

We all turned to stare at the little girl who usually said nothing. And while I liked her theory that Rex was on the job, I think I'd rather have the Basque Separatists.

"Hey, Merry-go-round!" Rex's father clapped me on the back.

Mike Ferguson, a large man with a mad scientist-y shock of black hair and a booming voice, had taken to giving me nicknames in the last couple of weeks. I wasn't fond of it, but I liked him too much to say anything. At least the holidays were over and he'd stopped calling me Merry Christmas.

"How're you holding up?" Millie, Rex's mother, looked worried. Petite and plump with dark hair streaked with silver, my future mother-in-law kept her fears to herself in an attempt to see how I was doing. I really liked her too.

"I'm fine," I lied. How could I feel sorry for myself when these people were worried?

"I think he skipped town!" Ronni shouted at my right elbow. "He didn't want to marry you and fled the country!"

"Ronni!" Randi snapped at her twin. "I'm sure that isn't what happened!"

The normally kind-hearted Millie shot her daughter a look that would've turned anyone else to stone. Ronni, who I was sure secretly fed on fear and fury, ignored it.

"Now we're not going to have a wedding," Ronni continued. "And I spent all week working on the haggis!"

The Fergusons were an unusual family, with Greek and Scottish ancestry. And they had some strange traditions that involved food—like me hand feeding the minister baklava and stepping on a haggis. Which made me wonder—why work all week on something I was only going to step on? Kelly had been worried that it would destroy my dainty, white satin, kitten heel (no, they're not made of kittens…I checked) shoes. So, I'd ordered a pair of custom wedding combat boots. It was kind of a win-win, really.

As for the Ferguson traditions, Rex and I had shot down some of the other stuff, like the sword fight between the bride and groom (the only thing I kind of liked), among other things. But we had to relent on the haggis. Do you know what haggis is?

It's the less attractive parts of a pig stuffed into a sheep's stomach.

"Ronni!" Randi snapped. "Merry has enough to worry about without you complaining about the haggis!"

That was true.

As the Fergusons dragged Ronni away and began to argue quietly in the corner, I looked around the church. The sheriff was kneeling next to the pew where the dead florist had been. The crime scene tape was still in place, and I couldn't help but wonder if that would be more appropriate for the pew bows, since murder seemed to follow me everywhere I went.

A frown came over Carnack's face, and I watched as he reached up under the seat and extracted something that fit in the palm of his hand. What was it?

Soo Jin had returned and appeared at my side with Kelly, who gently let me know that the pastor thought we should move things along.

"We could go ahead with the rehearsal," the coroner suggested. "Rex can figure it all out tomorrow." She patted me on the arm. "I'm sure he'll be here."

Kelly nodded. "I like that idea. And it will give everyone something to do."

With a sigh, I agreed. "Okay. Let's do it." Maybe it would be like that law of physics, where your food at a restaurant only arrived when you were in the bathroom. Would Rex magically appear like that once we started?

"The only thing is"—Kelly looked around—"we need a stand-in for Rex."

"How about Dad?" I shrugged

My matron of honor shook her head. "No, both of your parents are giving you away."

"Rex's dad?" I asked.

Soo Jin piped up. "He's giving the reading, remember? He can't be in two places at once."

I stared at them. "We have a *reading*?" I didn't tell them I had no idea what a reading was, because I didn't want to look like an idiot.

The only other men here who didn't have significant roles to play were Kevin, Sheriff Carnack, and...

"Riley!" Kelly shouted.

Oh no. Not him.

The newly (and somewhat questionably) minted private eye strolled up the aisle, and before I could say anything, agreed to be the stand-in for my missing groom. He held out his arm with a grin I couldn't quite interpret but definitely wanted to wipe off his face…with a cheese grater. I shoved him toward the altar and walked back to the entrance.

Kelly called for everyone to take their places, and for a brief moment in Bizarro World, I wondered if it really wouldn't be better to use Kevin Dooley instead.

My heart was pounding as Randi took her spot at the organ, with Ronni ready to turn the pages of music for her. Robert, Kelly's husband, played usher and escorted the Fergusons to their seats before taking his place with Riley at the front of the church.

In the doorway, the ten little girls lined up two-by-two and, once the music started, solemnly walked up the aisle, pretending to drop flower petals. Good thing this was just a rehearsal. With that many flower girls, I'd be wading through two feet of silk flowers to get to the altar.

Soo Jin waited for the last two girls to go before heading slowly up the aisle herself. Kelly gave me a wink before following her.

"Ready, kiddo?" Mom whispered.

Dad squeezed my hand.

"I'd be a lot more ready if Rex was here," I grumbled. Where *was* he?

As the processional began to play, we walked up the aisle. Passing row after row of empty pews looked strange against the altar-heavy church laden with ten flower girls and two bridesmaids.

And while I went through the motions of the ceremony, my mind was overrun with concern for Rex.

"Just like old times," Riley whispered. "Eh, Wrath?"

I glared at him. "I don't remember marrying you before now."

"You don't remember Oslo?"

The pastor cleared his throat to get us to stop talking.

I'd forgotten about Oslo. Riley and I had been posing as tourists in the Norwegian capital, complete with sham wedding and an even more shammy honeymoon. I shuddered, recalling the trolls who'd tossed mushrooms at us on the way out of the chapel. Riley had almost convinced me that it had been a real marriage after all—until I saw that the *marriage certificate* had been signed by Thor.

"You'd better not be behind this," I growled.

"I had nothing to do with Rex's disappearance," he insisted. "I'm as worried as you are."

*I'll bet.*

As the ceremony went on, everyone seemed eager to do their bit. Probably as a distraction from Rex's disappearance and the dead body, now at the morgue. Riley took my hand and kept squeezing it. I responded with a bone-crushing grip. He gasped a little, and I hoped that would be enough to deter him from the kiss at the end. That was *not* going to happen.

The rehearsal wrapped with the recessional, and as the girls giggled and looked back at us, I knew something was up. Were they planning something for the real thing? I wouldn't put it past them. I loved my troop of wonderfully precocious little girls. But if they were working together on some sort of prank, we were screwed.

"That went well," Kelly announced from the altar. "If I can just see the flower girls, bridesmaids, and parents for a moment..."

Everyone moved back to the front of the church as Sheriff Carnack joined Riley and me near the doorway.

"Any news?" I asked eagerly.

He shook his head. "Not yet. But my deputies are on it." He gave Kevin a long look. The officer was standing in the lobby, pretending to quick draw his gun on a statue of Saint Bernadette.

"Is he alright?" the sheriff asked.

I shook my head. "No. He's a danger to himself and others. I'd suggest you arrest him." Sadly, stupidity isn't a crime. "What are your deputies doing?"

Sympathy shone in his eyes. "Everything we can. I promise. In the meantime, I have a few questions about Mr. Spitz, the deceased."

He gave Riley a strange glance, and I introduced him. "This is Riley Andrews. He was my handler at the CIA, recently switched to the FBI out of Omaha, and now is starting up a PI firm."

The sheriff knew about my past. I'd had to let it slip during a fishing fiasco with my girls last spring.

Carnack's eyes grew wide. "Over in the strip mall? I wondered who that was." He held out his hand, and Riley took it. "Nice to meet you, Mr. Andrews. I'm impressed with your experience, but I don't think you'll be very busy here. Not with the police station and the sheriff's office in town."

Riley smiled warmly. "Thanks, Sheriff. I'm thinking of it as a sort of quasi-retirement."

"What can I do to help?" I interrupted the mutual admiration society. "Rex is missing, and my florist is dead."

Sheriff Carnack shrugged. "Anything you can do would be great."

My jaw dropped. Maybe I was just too used to hearing that I'd be in the way or was meddling. I'd expected him to shut me down.

The large man seemed to anticipate what I was thinking. "I'm responsible for the whole county, and we've just started an investigation into a meth ring in Bladdersly. You've got the skills to help investigate, and I'm going to need your help."

Of course there was a meth ring in Bladdersly. That unfortunately named town was a nefarious rival of Who's There. Every year the Whorish (an unfortunate blending of Who and Irish) battled the Raging Bladders in a tepid football game between two teams who were equally terrible. If I had to draw an analogy, I'd say it was like watching two dead flies circling a drain to see who went down first.

"Yes!" I said a little too quickly. "I'll do it! I'll help with Rex's disappearance. And if it's related, I can help with the murder investigation." I was not, however, asking to help with the meth ring in Bladdersly. I wasn't going anywhere near that hellhole if I could avoid it.

"The only thing is," he said slowly, "in law enforcement, whenever an officer has a personal connection to a case, they aren't allowed to investigate. But with your history as a resident and relationship to 99 percent of all murders here in town, I'm willing to overlook that."

"I can help too, Sheriff," Riley offered.

Carnack nodded. "Good. Because this murder is adding another problem to my plate. Did you know the deceased?"

Dr. Body left the front and joined us, sensing, I suppose, that her input would be needed.

I shook my head. "Not really. Kelly booked him. Or maybe my mother did. I'd met him once or twice. I guess he knew my grandmother, because he came out of retirement to help his son handle my flowers."

Whoa. Was the murder connected to Kelly or Mom and not me?

Rex's absence appeared to loosen Soo Jin's tongue. "Everything points to him being stabbed once through the heart. I haven't done a full autopsy, because I had to be here." She smiled warmly at me.

I remembered seeing Carnack take something from the crime scene. "Sheriff, what did you find under the pew?"

The man reached into his pocket and pulled out a piece of paper.

I nodded as I leaned in to read the note.
*Wedding traditions as good as gold...*
*Let's start out with Something Old.*

Lewis Spitz's death wasn't a random murder. The mention of the wedding made me realize an unfortunate truth.

This was aimed at me.

# CHAPTER THREE

———

"I'm afraid, Ms. Wrath," Sheriff Carnack apologized, "that I'll have to check the note for fingerprints."

As the sheriff turned to leave, he gave me one last look. "I'm sure Rex is okay. I'll do what I can to find him. In the meantime, I'll contact the station and let them know you're approved to work on the case."

"Approved?" My eyebrows went up. "No one is really in charge there now, right?"

He shook his head. "There are a few officers working there and a new detective trainee. I'll let them know." And with that, he left.

Rex had said something about them getting a new ambitious rookie. Was that who Carnack was talking about?

"Do you want me to cancel the rehearsal dinner?" Mom put her arm around me and nodded toward the Fergusons. We were supposed to go to their Greek restaurant, Syma's, in Des Moines.

"No," I said quickly. "What if Rex really is okay and planning to catch up to us later? He'll go there."

My mother smiled at me. "Of course. Good idea. I'll let everyone know."

The church emptied out pretty quickly. Either people were creeped out by the murder that had taken place there or eager to eat. My heart sank as the pastor handed Mom a card. Probably his number so we could call off the wedding tomorrow if we still hadn't heard from Rex.

It wasn't like I could get married without him. My parents and I paid for the whole event, but I didn't care about that right now. Finding Rex was my first priority. My next challenge would be convincing him that the sheriff invited me to work on the murder.

As I sat in the back seat of my parents' black SUV rental, I tried Rex's cell and my locating app again. Nothing. Where was he? He'd better have a good reason for freaking me out, or I was going to kill him.

For distraction, I turned my thoughts to Lewis Spitz. Why was he murdered? And in the church I was getting married in? No, why would he write the note that went with it? Unless he decided to commit suicide right there and leave us all hopelessly confused.

"Mom? Dad?" I called up to the front seat. "Did you guys know Leonard Spitz?"

My parents had grown up in Who's There. And since it was a small town and Spitz was the age of Methuselah and knew Grandma Wrath, they should know him.

"It's funny you should ask," Judith Czrygy said. "He did the flowers for our wedding."

I sat forward. "He did?"

She nodded. "He was a friend of my mother's. They'd known each other since they were five years old."

Dad piped up, "I think he was a second cousin or something like that. I'm not sure."

Dad's parents died years ago, and his family scattered to the four winds. I'm not kidding—his brother and sister and their families moved to Four Winds, Arkansas. They couldn't make it to the wedding but sent a nice cut-glass pitcher that I filled with cat treats.

"So," I surmised, "he was connected to both of you. And now, through this wedding, to me."

Which meant he wasn't connected to any number of international enemies I had. Unless this was all an attempt to mess up my wedding. It seemed like a petty thing, to sabotage a wedding of a former enemy. Why not just kill me?

And why leave the note? It certainly didn't frame me for the murder, like so many I'd been unfortunate to be around for the past three years.

"Do you think someone is just trying to scare you?" Dad said over his shoulder.

"If that's the case, murdering my florist is a bit over the top, don't you think?"

"Should I call the caterer? Or maybe the organist?" Mom sounded worried. "To make sure they're alright?"

I shrugged. "Maybe."

As she made her calls, I thought about that. The caterer was the owner of Oleo's, my favorite burger restaurant in town. And the organist was a beyond-geriatric woman with a stooped back, named Olive Clinton. She was the owner of Clinton's, one of two rival grocery stores in town.

"Everybody's fine," Mom said a few moments later with relief in her voice. "Olive's son is in town for the store's anniversary on January first, and Pat Barnes said everything is fine and all set for the reception tomorrow."

The question was, would there be a reception tomorrow?

*　*　*

Rex was not at Syma's.

I slumped a little as I scanned the room. Everyone else was there, which was strange because how did they all manage to beat me here? Even my troop was downing Shirley Temples at an alarming rate. We'd invited the parents, but every single one opted out. Maybe they just didn't like Greek food.

Where was Rex? And why couldn't I find him? I started walking around the room with my parents, making small talk with the guests. But my heart wasn't in it. It was out there, somewhere, with my fiancé.

"Detective Ferguson disappeared from the earth!" said one of the Kaitlyns as I approached them.

Ava shook her head. "He's somewhere. Everybody's somewhere. We just don't know where."

"He could be nowhere," Betty said as she nibbled on a breadstick. "Like in another dimension."

"Nobody is nowhere." Caterina rolled her eyes. "I think he's on a secret mission."

This made me smile. The girls loved Rex. In their eyes he was a super cop with supernatural abilities—one of which was endless patience for little girls. And no matter how many times I insisted that he didn't have X-ray vision, they refused to believe it.

"Mrs. Wrath!" Hannah shouted.

Apparently, the girls just realized I was standing next to them, and they turned to stare at me as if I'd sprouted two heads.

"It's okay, girls." I patted two of the Kaitlyns on the head. "Just checking in to see if you have everything."

"Are you going to get married tomorrow if Mr. Ferguson isn't here?" Lauren asked.

Caterina punched her in the arm. "Don't say that!"

Lauren shrugged. "You could have a marriage by proxy. Someone stands in for the groom. People did it in the olden days."

"Philby could do it." Betty gazed at her handiwork. She'd nibbled the breadstick into an impressive replica of a Bowie knife.

"Animals can't stand in!" Ava scowled. "That would be illegal!"

I was pretty sure marriage by proxy was illegal, but I was impressed that they knew that in the first place, so I let it slide.

"To answer your question," I said, "no, if there's no groom, there won't be a wedding. We'll just put it off for another date."

I really didn't want to do that. Planning for this wedding had seriously stressed me out—and I'd only been in charge of hiring the organist. I'd held auditions. Olive Clinton was the only one who knew how to play the *Dora the Explorer* theme music. And since I first spotted my future husband while peeking out from behind a pair of Dora bedsheets that I was using as living room curtains, it had been appropriate.

"We can help with a search party!" Inez clapped her hands.

"I've got snowshoes!" Ava nodded.

"We should wear camouflage," Betty added. "I bought a winter sniper ghillie suit online."

Of course she did.

"Thanks, girls," I said. "I'll let you know. For now, you should eat."

The room had tables formed in a U-shape. The girls were at one end of the U, with Kelly and Soo Jin next to them. The head table was where Rex and I would sit. I felt a little stab of pain when I saw his spot was empty. On the other side were my parents and Rex's family. The pastor and organist sat with them.

As I sat down in my spot, the empty one next to me seemed to draw attention to the fact that I was either alone and marrying myself or that my groom had achieved invisibility. Dinner was brought in on huge platters and placed on the tables, family-style.

Greek food was my third favorite, after Italian and junk. The tantalizing smells of stuffed grape leaves should've had me diving for my plate. But I wasn't hungry. I was worried. Missing the rehearsal was one thing…but the dinner too?

I had a terrible feeling I wasn't getting married in the morning.

"Are you going to be okay?" Riley said. He was sitting in the spot next to Rex's empty chair.

I turned to him. "You don't think there's a connection to the CIA, do you? An old enemy of mine who'd kidnap Rex?"

He thought for a moment. "I can make a call, if you'd like. Ahmed might know."

"Ahmed still owes me money for a case of peanut butter sandwich cookies from last year." My thoughts turned to the upcoming cookie sale. Fortunately, Kelly always handled that.

"Even better. He'll do it if you forgive his debt." Riley stood up and walked out of the room.

What could Ahmed find out? He was awfully low on the totem pole at Langley. Still, it was doing something. Sitting here wasn't going to find Rex. Maybe Riley could get some intel.

The fact that most of my enemies were dead or in prison was partly due to me. Midori Ito of the Yakuza was dead, and her daughter Leiko was in prison. Lana Babikova was in a penitentiary, and I'd run over Carlos the Armadillo. That was an accident. He just sort of flew at the front of my car while I was driving.

There were others…a strong man in Chechnya, a pair of twin albinos in Patagonia, among others. Riley could at least find out if they were in the country. And if they had Rex, I was going to kill them.

"You have to eat something." Kelly spooned ziti onto my plate.

"That's true," I mumbled but made no move to pick up my fork. "I have to keep my energy up, just in case."

My best friend added bread and fruit to my plate. "In case what?"

"In case there's a fight. Or a car chase. I need to be ready."

Kelly shook her head. "He's fine. You won't need to fight or chase anyone. Something's off, I agree. But let's not jump to conclusions just yet."

"And Lewis Spitz?" I lowered my voice. "The poem about his murder being connected to me?" I repeated the rhyme.

Kelly sat back. "I think someone's just trying to scare you."

"My money's on Juliette Dowd," I grumbled.

Juliette Dowd was a psycho who worked for the Girl Scouts and made my life a living hell. Why? Because she thought she should be with Rex. When she couldn't have him, I became her favorite target.

Don't get me wrong—I loved our local council. Every other employee was amazing. Exceptional. It was just this one woman who made things difficult for me. But could she have taken Rex? At least if she had, she wouldn't hurt him. She might trick him into marrying her, but I could handle that.

I plotted my revenge on the angry redhead through dinner and the drive home. My parents were staying with me. Mom took care of the cats as Dad walked over and collected Leonard.

As I lay in bed that night, I hoped I was dreaming. That I'd wake up and it would be this morning and Rex would be here and my florist would be alive. With that in mind, I managed to fall asleep.

# CHAPTER FOUR

———

"Fionnaghuala Czrygy!"

I knew that voice. There was only one person on the planet, who wasn't either of my parents, who knew how to pronounce my name (sounds like "Finella Scissorgee"). Almost everyone else called me Finn C.

Mrs. Willard's measured voice was firm, in spite of the unspoken exclamation mark. She was my fourth-grade teacher and one of my favorite people, but she didn't tolerate nonsense. Which made me think that for some reason, I was now committing said nonsense.

I looked around the classroom. Kelly, on my left, was wiggling her eyebrows meaningfully. Not that I understood what she was trying to say. Had I fallen asleep in class? Was she telling me I was dead meat? She probably was. Kelly told me that a lot.

Kevin Dooley was on my right, attempting to discreetly eat paste. Most kids give that up in kindergarten, but Kevin was kind of a slow learner. He didn't even make eye contact. His gaze was on the teacher. The boy never noticed anyone except for the person who could make him stop eating.

"Yes, Mrs. Willard?" I asked cautiously.

I never fell asleep in class. So why did I feel like I'd just magically appeared at my desk midday?

The teacher looked at me expectantly for a moment before answering. "In *From the Mixed-Up Files of Mrs. Basil E. Frankweiler*"—she took a breath. It was a long book title—"what do you think of Claudia's actions? Of running away with her brother?"

Ah. E. L. Konigsburg's book was one of my favorites, and like the children in the story, I'd always fantasized about running off to live in a famous museum (unlike the children, I'd never done that…yet). Not that I had any reason to run away from home. My parents were totally cool. But leaving Who's There, Iowa, and Kevin Dooley behind me would be a plus.

It was my teacher's favorite book too. I glanced at her desk to see a stack of crossword puzzles sandwiched between a couple of Sherlock Holmes books. This story of two little kids who attempt to solve an art mystery was one of the few books I'd heard she taught every single year.

"Oh!" I shouted, causing Kevin to drop his bottle of paste. He left it on the floor at his feet, as if he didn't know it existed, and pulled something I *hoped* was a Milk Dud from his pants pocket and popped it into his mouth.

My voice wavered a little. "I think she was right. I'd love to live in a museum."

The class snickered, and I wondered if I'd said the wrong thing. I shot a glance at my best friend for encouragement, and she smiled and nodded. Kelly was super amazing. She'd run away with me to a museum.

Mrs. Willard did not nod with approval or criticize my answer. "What would you think would be the equivalent to the Metropolitan Museum of Art here?"

I chewed on my pencil for a moment. "The Des Moines Museum of Art. Or the zoo. I like the zoo."

The kids laughed as the teacher finally nodded. She turned to another student, and the heat was off of me.

"Good answer!" Kelly whispered, giving me a thumbs-up.

I couldn't help but smile. I was warming up to the idea that she and I could run away sometime. Just for a little adventure. Not forever or anything. I looked at my teacher and realized she was a lot like Mrs. Basil E. Frankweiler in the book. Firm but approachable, Mrs. Willard always said that kids would perform exactly how you expected them to.

I wasn't totally sure what that meant. But since we all worked harder in her class than in any other, I guessed it was a good thing.

"Mrs. Wrath!" someone wailed behind me.

That was weird. Was my grandmother here? She was the only Mrs. Wrath in town. I turned to face a scowling girl who I'd never seen before. Wait…that wasn't entirely true. I *did* know her. How did I know her?

"Mrs. Wrath!" The girl shouted this time, and I flinched. As awesome as Linda was, she wasn't going to be happy at all about someone speaking out of turn, let alone doing it with their *outside* voice.

\*   \*   \*

My eyes flew open. Betty looked down at me. I'd been dreaming. In bed.

Sitting straight up, I searched the room for my co-leader. When I heard her voice in the living room, I ran to her. It was then I realized that the whole troop was in my house. And I was in my pajamas.

Oh right. Mom mentioned something last night about a search party! Sadness twisted my gut because the girls being here meant there was no news about Rex. Today was supposed to be our wedding day. But if Rex hadn't turned up by now, there wasn't going to be a wedding.

I had an idea. "Kelly! I know who we need!" I shook her arm.

My now grown-up best friend looked at me with sympathy. "How are you feeling? You don't have to go today."

I ignored her question. "I know who can help us!"

Kelly looked around. The girls were making posters, using pictures of Rex. Well, Lauren and Inez were drawing a picture of Rex as a unicorn princess, swathed in pink glitter that said, *LOST! Please return to Mrs. Wrath's house ASAP!*

"Merry," my friend said. "We've got half the town searching, along with the police department and the county sheriff's office."

Nodding quickly, I interrupted. "We need someone who's smart and practical. Someone who's amazing at puzzles. That's what the clue was! A puzzle!"

Kelly cocked her head to one side and arched her right eyebrow. She was waiting for me to explain.

"Mrs. Willard! We need her!"

"Our fourth-grade teacher?" Kelly placed the back of her hand on my forehead to see if I was feverish.

"Yes! She can help!"

Kelly shook her head. "You haven't gotten any sleep since yesterday."

"I just slept! That's how I came up with the idea! I had a dream about her!"

"Seems legit." Betty appeared at our side. "That's where most of my ideas come from." She handed us a poster for information leading to finding Rex that featured a four-million-dollar reward. Rex was dressed like a cowboy with a handlebar mustache. The girl gave us a wink and walked away.

\* \* \*

As I showered and got dressed, the idea made more and more sense to me. My former teacher was a whiz at puzzles. In fact, there'd been a number of stories in the local paper about how she'd won several puzzle competitions in the last couple of years since her retirement. Sudoku, crosswords, and brainteasers were her favorite. If anyone could make sense of the message from the killer, she was that person!

"Come on!" I tugged on Kelly's sleeve. "I found her address in the phone book. We should go right now."

Kelly frowned. "The girls are here."

Ten little girls looked at each other and screamed with glee. There was no way I was leaving them alone in my house. They'd either dye my cat pink or burn my house to the ground.

"What about Mom?" I asked, looking around until I spotted her in the kitchen. "She and Dad can entertain them."

Mom agreed and sent Dad out for a bucket of cookie dough. I felt bad leaving her like that. Especially since I didn't even own a cookie sheet. Still, Mom was very resourceful (I'd seen her take a banquet with food for eight and turn it into a sumptuous feast for thirty, using nothing more than a toothpick and nail file). She'd think of something.

"We haven't seen Mrs. Willard in years," Kelly mumbled. "This might be the dumbest idea you've ever come up with."

That was saying something. I was pretty sure my best friend had a list of ideas she'd ruled out over the years. From sniper training camp to a field trip to Beirut, my suggestions were usually ignored.

I brushed her insult aside. "I saw her at Oleo's a week ago."

"Did you talk to her?" she asked.

I shook my head. "No, but it was definitely her."

"What if she doesn't remember us?"

"That's possible, I suppose." It had been a long time since the fourth grade. "I think she'll at least consider it."

It took only a moment to find her address in the phone book. The small brick condo was near the library. Pulling into the driveway, the fog cleared and I realized that this was a crazy idea. I ignored it, like I usually do when that happens. I ran to the house and knocked.

The door opened, and a petite, trim woman with short blonde hair answered. I couldn't believe it. She hadn't aged a single day. Now that I was here, I froze. Suddenly, this didn't seem like a great idea. I was freaking out—it was up to my best friend to keep me from making crazy decisions, wasn't it?

"Mrs. Willard?" Kelly asked tentatively. "I'm sure you don't remember us, but…"

"Finn Czrygy and Kelly Swanson," the woman answered with a knowing nod.

How did she remember Kelly's maiden name? She'd been Albers for years. And my name certainly didn't trip off the tongue.

"You remember us?" I asked. How did she remember us? I was very unremarkable as a child, but maybe because my father was a senator, she remembered me?

The retired teacher smiled. "I remember those students who I knew were going to do well in life."

She knew we'd do well? How did she get that from my miserable attempts at multiplication? Maybe it was because of my reading skills?

Kelly explained, "Well, sure, Merry became a spy and was famous when she was outed. But I'm just a nurse."

Mrs. Willard cocked her head to one side, "Just a nurse? You are an excellent nurse. You help people every day. I'd say that's successful."

I'd forgotten how straightforward the woman was. If she thought something was important to do, she did it. If she had something to say, she said it. Most Iowans were known for their brisk, matter-of-fact manner. But this was part of who Linda was, and I'd always admired her straight talk.

We must've been staring, because she said, "You remember me. Why shouldn't I remember you?"

I threw my arms around her. "You were my favorite teacher!"

The woman chuckled softly and hugged me back for a brief moment before pulling away.

"So, why are you here? I doubt that this is a social visit." There was that directness again.

Kelly and I looked at each other before I responded, "I have a huge problem. And I think you're the one to help me solve it."

Our fourth grade teacher looked us in the eyes for a few seconds before nodding. "Then I guess you'd better come in."

We followed her inside, and I thought about everything I knew (which wasn't much) about my retired teacher. She'd been married and widowed young and had a daughter who had to be an adult by now. She was tenacious. I remember my dad at the kitchen table, reading the paper and praising Mrs. Willard for the job she did, representing the local teachers in negotiations with the administration. A real tiger, he'd called her. I could use a real tiger about now.

"Please." She motioned to a comfy sofa in a cozy room, and we sat. "Can I get you anything? Tea or cookies?"

I shook my head, "No thank you. We don't mean to impose. And I'm sorry we dropped by so suddenly."

The woman smiled broadly, making us feel at home. "You don't need to apologize. I'm happy you're here. Now, what can I do for you?"

Wow. I'd expected confusion (something I'm known for causing) and some resistance. She offered neither.

"My fiancé has been kidnapped." It all came out in one whooshing breath.

I told her the whole story, with Kelly filling in where I'd left something out. We talked about Lewis Spitz's murder, of Rex's disappearance, and the bizarre clue left by the body. She never gasped or freaked out, just listened patiently, nodding to offer encouragement.

Most people are terrible listeners. They talk a good game but never get around to asking how you are. Mrs. Willard was silently supportive. As I spoke, I felt a sense of hope. This woman could handle anything. I wanted her on my side.

Empathy shone in her eyes. "I'm so sorry, Merry. It sounds like you've been through a lot in the last twenty-four hours. How can I help?"

I hesitated and looked at Kelly, who nodded. "I need your talent with puzzles. I need your help."

"May I see the clue?" she asked without a moment's pause, and I knew that I'd come to the right person.

I'd written down the verse from the clue we'd found near Spitz and offered it up. Linda took the slip and read it aloud.

"Wedding traditions as good as gold...Let's start out with Something Old. It's from that old wedding rhyme," she said almost immediately. "Something old, something new, something borrowed, and something blue."

"Wait! There's a wedding rhyme?" I asked.

Kelly stared at me. I guess I should've known that. Mrs. Willard simply nodded and explained.

"Those are all things a bride should have with her on her wedding day."

She looked thoughtfully into space before saying, "Mr. Spitz was the something old. You'll be getting one about something new, next, I imagine."

I hadn't thought about that. I'd been so wrapped up in Rex's disappearance that I hadn't given the possibility of another clue any real thought.

"That means Rex is still alive!" I did inner dialogue cartwheels—which was way better than actual cartwheels.

She nodded. "I think so. My guess is you'll have until the last clue to find him. It doesn't seem like there'll be a request for a ransom. This person wants to see if you're up to the task to match wits with them."

"I'm not up to the task! I didn't even think about a ransom! Would you help us?" My words bubbled over, tripping on my tongue.

"Merry," Kelly chastised. "I don't think you should drag Mrs. Willard into this…"

Our former teacher interrupted, "It's Linda, and of course I will."

"Wait," I said. "You didn't correct Kelly when she called me Merry."

Linda nodded. "I know you go by Merry Wrath now. I just used your real name at the door because I wanted you to know that I remembered you."

She was sharp as a tack. We definitely needed her!

"Thank you!" I gushed.

Linda stood. "I'm looking forward to it. As soon as you get another clue, let me know."

We got to our feet, and I threw my arms around her again. Kelly was appalled. I didn't care. I was so happy to have her on our side, I couldn't contain myself.

*　*　*

"I can't believe she remembered us," Kelly mused as I backed the van out of the driveway.

"I can't believe she's going to help us!" I said. "She's so smart. We'll find Rex in no time!"

Kelly looked at me. "You don't have to join the search party, you know."

"Of course I do!" I pulled into the parking lot of Ferguson Taxidermy—Where Your Pet Lives On Forever! This was Ronni and Randi's shop, and they offered it up as HQ for Operation Find the Fiancé. Well, Randi did.

The lot was packed, which made my heart swell. One thing I loved about small towns was how people pulled together in a crisis. That and Rice Krispies Treats at potlucks. But mostly the pulling-together thing.

Inside the large Victorian house was a crush of people gawking at various dioramas of animals dressed like people, doing people-y things. The newest attraction appeared to be a mountain lion, in top hat and tails, waltzing with an emu dressed as a hippie. It was pretty impressive, especially with the all-warthog orchestra.

"Merry!" Dr. Body threw her arms around me, crushing me in the process. She smelled like roses and vanilla because...of course she did. "So many came out to help!"

Soo Jin took my hand and led me through the crush of people, past four coyotes dressed as Disney Villains, past a hawk wearing a slinky red dress and high heels, and past a group of snakes playing Monopoly. How did they hold their cards without arms? I stopped for a moment to linger, but the coroner yanked hard, so I kept going. I made a mental note to ask Randi how much that piece was.

We arrived in a small library that, to my surprise, didn't have one single dead animal in it. The fact that there was a completely normal room in this house made my jaw drop.

"I picked this room for the nerve center," Soo Jin said as she looked at the floor-to-ceiling bookcases. "It seemed...quieter somehow."

A man in a police uniform stepped in. He was young, maybe twenty-two, and carried a stack of file folders. He laid them down on the table in the middle of the room and pulled up a chair. We followed suit.

"This is Officer Weir," Dr. Body said. "He joined the force a few months ago and offered to help." She leaned forward and whispered, "I figured he was better than having Officer Dooley assist."

Kelly and I nodded vigorously. Officer Ted Weir was a good-looking kid, with brown hair, green eyes, and a warm smile. So this was the new guy I'd heard about. The question was, would he be up to this challenge? He wasn't a detective, but everyone starts somewhere, I supposed.

"I'm so sorry this happened, Ms. Wrath," he said as he shook our hands. "I know I've only been here a short time, but I look up to Detective Ferguson. He's a good man."

There was that knot in my stomach again, and my throat ached. At least he used present tense. If he'd used past tense, I'd have probably lost it.

"Thank you," I croaked out. I was probably going to lose it anyway.

"What's in the files?" Kelly said quickly. She knew I was about to cry and distracted me. I was so lucky to have a friend like her.

"These," Ted said, "are people Detective Ferguson locked up. I figure this is a good starting point."

Whoa. I'd been so sure this was about me that I never thought about the fact that it could be someone connected to Rex. The poem wasn't necessarily specific to me. Was I so self-absorbed that I'd missed this? What else had I missed?

Soo Jin and Kelly helped themselves to a few folders off the top, but my mind was racing. Was this all about revenge against Rex? If so, I was hopelessly out of my league. Rex didn't discuss many cases with me, and sadly I realized that I'd never asked. I had no idea where to even start.

Spies are used to having enemies, and I'd had plenty over the years. But policemen had them too. I'd forgotten that. And by doing so could've screwed up the investigation, putting Rex in even more danger.

"Here's one!" Soo Jin squealed. "Harvey Oak. Says he ran a chop shop in a barn outside of town." She frowned. "Who's There had a chop shop?"

It surprised me too. That sounded more like something that would happen in that raging hellhole known as Bladdersly. "Is he in prison?"

"No." She shook her head, and every hair in her glossy black bob unfairly fell right back into place. "It says he was paroled last month. Did two years though, and Rex put him away. It looks like it was one of his first cases here."

Ted nodded. "I also have cases from the city he worked in before he came here. Davenport, Iowa. He's only been here a few years, so I thought I'd go further back."

Rex worked in Davenport? How did I not know that?

"This guy shows promise," Kelly said. "Prescott Winters III. He murdered his wealthy wife and dumped her in the Mississippi. Got out after four years on good behavior. No priors."

Two bad guys? We had two suspects who wanted to hurt Rex?

"Don't forget Vy Todd," Ted said.

I snatched the file out of his hands. "Vy Todd? Rex made that arrest?"

Everyone in Iowa…and everywhere else…knew about Vy Todd. Five years ago, before I was outed as a spy, I'd heard about it while hiding out in a yurt in Mongolia. It had excellent Wi-Fi. Anyway, Vy masterminded a vast smuggling network, using the Mississippi River as a main artery. There were a number of murders tied to her, but the police had no evidence.

Mostly she'd smuggled drugs up from Louisiana, on barges she bribed. In almost every case, she'd never appeared to be directly involved. Which was why it was so weird that she'd got caught in a canoe loaded with heroin in the middle of the river in the middle of the night. It was a rare catch, and the papers had tagged her the Crack Catfish. She never did the dirty work. But her number one guy had been sick with the flu, and she'd gone to meet the barge in his place.

Kelly's eyes grew wide. "She promised to kill the police detective who found her out."

"And that detective," Ted said, "was Rex Ferguson."

"And that smuggler"—I pointed to the page—"just got pardoned by the governor one month ago."

"She relocated to Des Moines," Ted added. "Last week. Local law enforcement paid her a little visit to let her know they were watching her."

Vy Todd—a vicious, dangerous smuggler and possible murderer.

"Where does she live?" I asked through gritted teeth.

# CHAPTER FIVE

————

Ted Weir and Dr. Body exchanged glances.

"I don't think that's a good idea," Kelly said slowly. "Maybe the police should talk to her."

It sounded like Kelly was worried about me challenging an extremely hostile felon. But I knew her and was fairly certain she was worried about me going to jail for murdering Vy Todd. Silly woman. I wouldn't get caught. There were lots of ways to make a murder look like an accident—using a car crash, drug overdose, or finding a poisonous water snake in your bath. And while the last example was a tad bit questionable, I made a mental note to look up poisonous snakes of Iowa with bubble bath fetishes.

"I'll call Des Moines," Officer Weir said. "See what they know. They might even have her under surveillance." He stood and collected the files.

I grabbed a notepad off the desk and made a few notes.

"Wait until you hear something from Officer Weir, Merry," Soo Jin said gently.

I looked at each one of them in turn. Finally, I gave in. "Fine. But if he doesn't find something soon, I'm going to pay all of these people a special visit." I left out that my travelling companion might be a venomous snake.

It was dark outside when Kelly and I made our way to my van. The girls and citizens of Who's There had plastered posters everywhere during the day, and we passed many a picture of Rex as a sparkly unicorn, and one of him shooting lasers out of his eyes at something that looked suspiciously like Basque Separatists.

Kelly hugged me the minute we got back to my house, before heading home.

I unlocked the house and found two cats and a dog sitting in the foyer, in a row, staring at me.

"Mom? Dad?" I called out, but there was no answer.

Had they gone to stay at the Radisson? I could understand if they had. A moment later I had my answer with a note on the fridge that told me my parents were picking up groceries. That was probably a good idea. My parents wouldn't be able to subsist on Lucky Charms and Pizza Rolls.

Philby and Martini jumped onto the counter. Philby, a Hitler look-alike, if Hitler were obese and suspiciously hairy, wasn't having any of it. Whatever "it" was. She glared at me to remind me that I'd been gone too long and didn't I know she was in charge here?

Her kitten, a now young cat named Martini, looked like Elvis and had the tendency to fall asleep anywhere at any time in a matter of seconds. She wasn't sleeping now. She was right there, next to her mother, giving me the stink eye.

Stink eye. Oh, right. Food. The girls wanted their albacore tuna. Right. Now.

I fed the cats, herded Leonard outside, and prepared his dinner. Once they were all eating, I collapsed onto the couch. In spite of the darkness, the curtains were open, and I could see the dark, lonely outline of Rex's house across the street.

Actually it was now my house. Well, it would have been if I'd gotten married today. Rex had been pressing me for a while to sell mine, but I just couldn't. It was my first real home, and I loved it. His was a larger saltbox-style house with two floors, in comparison with my one-level ranch. I got that moving into his house made more sense. I just didn't want to abandon mine.

I'd decided a few days ago to keep it as a sort of Girl Scout clubhouse where I stored my spy gear and weaponry I didn't want Rex to know I had. I was going to broach the subject after our honeymoon.

The honeymoon! Did Mom cancel it? I hoped so. Even so, the thought of it made me sad.

We'd been planning it for months. I'd suggested the beaches of Thailand or Honduras, but Rex was more traditional and wanted to go to the Bahamas. I relented because I wanted him to be happy.

I texted Mom and asked her if she'd cancelled it. She responded back immediately, agreeing and that she and Dad would be home soon. The thought of food sounded nice, but I didn't think I could eat. Exhaustion was creeping into my bones. I was heartsick and physically tired.

My name should be Merry Ferguson right now. But it wasn't. I was still Merry Wrath, single woman.

Leonard jumped onto the couch and climbed awkwardly onto my lap. We'd been working on stopping this behavior because I looked like a daddy longlegs spider with a rat sitting on me. The dog settled and whimpered, nosing my hand for attention.

Not to be outdone, Philby jumped onto the back of the couch and settled around my shoulders like a living fur stole. Martini looked at us, belched, and trotted toward the bedroom. I thought she had the right idea.

Somewhere along the line, I passed out. I think my parents came home and tried to wake me but gave up. My body was melded to the couch. Getting up now, even to go to my room, would probably result in me not being able to sleep for the rest of the night, so I stayed put.


I woke up a few hours later. My legs had gone to sleep and were wet with dog drool, and my shoulders felt like they were being crushed. I gently nudged the animals off of me. Actually, I kind of slid out from under them as they slept.

I stood up, and forgetting that my legs were asleep, fell over. Getting myself into a sitting position on the floor, I rubbed both legs vigorously in an attempt to regain feeling and in hopes of someday walking again.

Out of the corner of my eye, I saw a flicker of light out the window. Probably just car headlights. We lived on the corner of an intersection. I reached up and turned off the lamp before forcing my legs into a standing position. A tingling sensation ran the length of my muscles, and I regained use.

There was that flicker again. I stared at it out the window. There was a light. And it was coming from Rex's living room! He was home!

I'd never moved so quickly in my life. By the time my front door clicked shut behind me, I was across the street, walking up the driveway to Rex's house. The front door was slightly open, but it wouldn't have stopped me if it was locked.

I slid into the front hall just as the light in the living room on my right went out. I was beginning to regret my laziness at having Rex install a switch upstairs that controlled the lights downstairs. It seemed like a genius idea at the time, but now the fact that I couldn't be bothered to go downstairs and turn the lights out was coming back to haunt me.

Excitement turned to fear as I dropped to the floor and waited. What was I doing? I knew better than to charge into an unknown situation half-cocked. All I could do was listen. If it was Rex, we'd have a laugh about this, after I let him have it.

But if it wasn't, I needed to be prepared to handle whatever came my way. Were the kidnappers back? If so, they were soon going to be dead kidnappers.

Footsteps moved impatiently upstairs. Someone was going from room to room, throwing open drawers and closets. They made no other sound, so I couldn't tell if it was a man or woman.

Whoever it was, they only had one way out of the house—the stairs. Or the window if I surprised them. The fact that they'd be thrown *through* it instead of climbing out of it was a small detail.

This left me with two choices—going upstairs or waiting until they came down. I was pretty sure it was only one person. Not that it mattered. I could take down a charging elephant at this point.

The footfalls stopped. There was no sound for a second or two. That made my decision for me as I quietly mounted the stairs. The inner boards often creaked, so I kept my feet to one side or the other as I made my way toward the second floor.

I was kinda-sorta living here now, while still keeping my house across the street until I decided what to do with it. Rex and I had redone the bedroom so it wasn't so masculine. He drew the line at *Dora the Explorer* sheets though. And half of the stuff in the bathroom was now mine. But at this point, I still lived across the street, and my last name was still Wrath.

As my eyes came level with the next floor, I noticed it was dark. Did the intruder have a flashlight? If so, why turn on the living room light earlier? That didn't make any sense. It could be a stupid criminal, which was my personal favorite.

What if this wasn't the kidnapper at all? What if it was just a random burglary? The wedding notice had been in the paper, and according to that, we'd be out of the country by now. Bad guys often robbed houses after a wedding because there were usually a lot of gifts there. Which was why all of ours were in my basement, surrounded by booby traps.

Gifts. We'd registered at a department store in Des Moines. That was a fun day. After picking out a giant flamingo statue and forks that looked like trees, Rex gently took me off the detail, instead giving me one assignment. The collapsible TV tray tables. I spent hours winnowing it down to two different sets. One was dark mahogany, and the other was modern steel with blaze orange plastic tops. In the end, Rex chose the wood set. Said it matched the wood floors in the living room. He didn't know that I secretly bought the orange ones and had them sent to my house.

A grunt of frustration brought me back to the task at hand. The closet door in the guest room closed with a click. So that was where the bastard was. Very carefully, I made my way up the rest of the stairs and down the hall until I was right outside the door to that room.

Now what? I didn't have a weapon on me. I'd left the house too soon for that. And Rex most likely had his service weapon on him. And if he hadn't, it would take too much time to retrieve it from our bedroom closet, and there was the risk that I'd make noise in the process.

Our bedroom closet.

I started to choke up. *Focus, Merry! Someone's in your house!* That was all it took to change melancholy to murderously angry.

Footsteps moved toward me, and I plastered myself to the wall outside the room. A dark shadow stepped through the doorway, and once past me, I grabbed the intruder's arm, bent it behind his back, and shoved him face first into the wall.

The satisfying crunch and scream was definitely female. I flicked on the hall light with my other hand, and there, standing in a position I'd often fantasized about, was none other than Juliette Dowd.

# CHAPTER SIX

———

"Get off of me!" the angry redhead shrieked. She side-eyed me and shrieked again. "I'll sue you for assault and battery!"

I released her. "After breaking into my house in the middle of the night? Not likely."

The woman spun around and faced me. She was wearing a black turtleneck sweater, black leather jacket, black gloves, and black pants tucked into black boots. Hardly the right fashion choice to say she was just in the neighborhood and stopped by.

"You took Rex?" I asked through gritted teeth. "Where is he? If you've hurt him, I'm going to kill you and make sure the body is never, ever found."

Juliette shook her head furiously. "I didn't take him! I thought you'd killed him! That's why I came over here! To find proof so I could have you arrested!"

The thought of Officer Kevin Dooley showing up to arrest me, his hand arm deep in a box of Twinkies, although amusing, would take forever.

"Why"—I threw my arms in the air—"would I kill Rex?"

"Because you didn't love him!" Juliette shrieked.

"If I didn't love him, I'd just call off the wedding," I replied. "Why kill him? That doesn't make sense."

"You wanted his house!" She bit her lip, her voice a little less shrieky.

"I have a house! Across the street!" This was getting tiresome. "You really thought I was responsible for his disappearance?"

She nodded, but it lacked confidence.

"Why?" I asked.

"Because you found out he loves me." Big, watery tears rolled down her face.

I kind of felt sorry for her.

"If he told me he loved you and not me, I wouldn't stand in his way. I want him to be happy." This might've been a bit of a lie, but there wasn't any point in being mean to her. The woman, Satan or not, was suffering.

She snapped, defiantly, "Are you going to have me arrested?"

The idea of Kevin throwing the cuffs on her was tempting.

"No. I would like to know how you got in here though."

Juliette handed me a key.

"Where did you get this?" I turned it over in the light. It was a key to this house alright.

"Ronni," was all she said.

I was going to have to have a little chat with my future sisters-in-law.

"Get out," I said as I rubbed my eyes. "It's late, and I'm too tired to kill you."

She had a look on her face that implied she'd come back in a few hours, once I was fast asleep.

"If I come over here again tonight," I threatened, "I will do something you'll regret."

It was difficult to understand if she believed me. But the speed with which she fled gave me some inkling that she was done for the night. I walked through the bedrooms, closing drawers and picking up the things Juliette had tossed on the floor.

I lingered for a moment in the entryway before leaving and locking the door behind me. I was too tired to think straight. Juliette's break-in left me confused and conflicted.

Back in my bed, with Leonard curled up on the floor and the cats next to me, I wondered what to do with Juliette Dowd. Either she was holding Rex hostage and came over to steal something, or she genuinely thought I had something to do with his disappearance. Either way, it was too weird to be ignored.

* * *

"What are you doing?" Kelly tapped on my car window several hours later.

I unlocked the door and let her in. "I'm surveilling Juliette Dowd."

Kelly looked around the neighborhood that was across the street from the hospital, where she worked.

"Why?"

I glared at her through red eyes. "She broke into Rex's house last night. It's possible she's behind his disappearance." I pointed at a small white ranch house two doors down from where I was parked. "That's her house."

"How did you find out where she lived?" Kelly asked. She seemed slightly appalled.

I shrugged. "Freedom of Information Act." She started to speak, but I continued, "That and a friend at Langley got it for me." I was going to owe Ahmed more cookies in a month, but it was worth it.

Kelly rolled her eyes. "You seriously think she's got Rex in there?"

I shook my head, "No. I've already been inside. I think she has him stashed somewhere else."

My best friend's jaw dropped. "You broke in and looked around her house?"

"Well, duh. How else was I going to find him? My X-ray imaging device is broken."

"What's this?" She took my cell from me. "Poisonous snakes of Iowa?"

I looked at her through bleary, sleep-deprived eyes. "It's always good to have a plan B."

She closed the window on my cell and handed it back to me. "Merry." She sighed. "Go home. Get some sleep. Ted and Soo Jin are on this."

I narrowed my eyes. "Yeah. I was thinking about that. Thought I'd pay a visit to Vy Todd this afternoon."

"You can't do that!"

"Of course I can. It's a free country, and I know where she lives." Oddly, Ahmed was able to get me the smuggler's address before the Girl Scout employee's. "I have the perfect cover—selling Girl Scout Cookies."

"I'm not going to let you do that," Kelly said. "Look at you! You're exhausted, haven't slept, and are stalking people. You need some rest."

I shook my head. "I don't have time. Who knows what kind of place they have Rex locked up in! Maybe there's no heat! Or no food! I have to do what I can!"

"Merry." Uh-oh. Kelly was using her menacing nurse voice. "I'm going to follow you back to your house, and I'm calling your parents." She got out of the car and closed the door. "Now, drive!" she shouted through the window.

She was going to rat me out to my parents? That was a low blow. Kelly never did anything like that when we were kids. Why start now? As for the snakes, she was too late. I'd already placed an order for a timber rattlesnake.

I was so mad, I drove all over town before finally pulling into my driveway. She had to go to work and would be late, which was more than a little mean of me, but I was too spent to care. Mom opened the door when we pulled in. Dad was right behind her, looking worried.

Once Kelly marched me inside, she told my parents everything, which I thought was a bit unnecessary, and left.

Mom didn't say much as she marched me down to my room. She checked the windows to make sure they were locked before forcing me to get into bed. I did what I was told, because my new captors had to let their guard down sometime. I just needed to wait…

\* \* \*

"Good morning, kiddo!" Mom's cheerful voice roused me as she flung open the curtains of my bedroom.

"What the…" I mumbled as I avoided opening my eyes. My head was pounding, and my mouth was dry.

"Wait…" I said as my eyes flew open. "Morning?"

My mother nodded. "You slept for twenty-four hours!"

"What? How?" I rarely got more than seven hours and two minutes' worth of sleep. I don't know why that number, but that amount of time was all I needed.

She looked sheepish. "I might have drugged you. A bit."

I sat straight up, causing the pounding in my head to turn to all-out thunder. "Drugged me?"

Mom shrugged. "I found this bottle among your old spy stuff in the basement." She held up a bottle of Rohypnol.

Dammit! I was saving that! "You roofied me? You could've killed me!"

She laughed. "I highly doubt it. I figured out just the right amount."

"Dad!" I shouted at the top of my lungs.

Senator Mike Czrygy popped his head in with a jovial grin. "Can I make you breakfast?"

"Mom drugged me! She drugged me!" I howled.

Dad came over and sat down on the bed, patting my hand. "It's alright, munchkin. We thought it would help."

My parents were going through my dangerous spy stuff, came across a bottle of capsules, and doped me with it? How? I didn't remember eating or drinking anything yesterday.

"Kelly came over with some sedatives after her shift," Mom said brightly. "She cleared whatever was in there. Said you'd have a headache though."

My jaw dropped open. "I can't believe the three of you drugged me!"

"Well, you were emotionally and physically wiped out and kept referring to ordering snake venom. We thought some sleep would give you a fresh start when you woke up," Dad explained.

Mom nodded. "We didn't think you'd be out for an entire day, but that was an added bonus."

Dad got up and nodded to Mom. "Chocolate chip pancakes and bacon will be up in a few minutes. Take your time." And with that, they both left.

It took me a few minutes to recover from the shock that my parents and best friend gave me drugs without asking me. I staggered out of bed and into the shower. After ten minutes, I felt a little better. Soon I was dressed and at the breakfast bar, where my parents, dog, and cats were.

Leonard was eating from a bowl of kibbles on the floor, and the cats stared at the bacon expectantly. I covered the plate with a cloth napkin. Philby loved meat of any kind. And that included bacon. Once, she was so mad that we hadn't given her any, she walked slowly over the strips, making sure her paw hit each one. She then sat on the other side and waited for us to give her the bacon. For the record, I didn't want to, but Rex declared the plate a health hazard.

The smell of the food was too much, and I succumbed to eight pancakes and six strips of bacon before I found the power to talk.

"What's going on with the case? Is there any news? Has Rex appeared?" I thought this unlikely or he'd be here, arresting my parents for doping me.

Mom held up her hands. "Nothing yet, but Officers Weir and Dooley should be here any moment to brief us."

That sounded sort of promising. If there was going to be a briefing, that meant they knew something, right? I was so encouraged, I ate five more pancakes. You should never investigate on an empty stomach. Once, in Japan, I'd skipped two meals during a surveillance and had to go with the closest thing, which was raw squid from a street vendor. I'd never been that sick before or after, and the guy I was following got away.

"I'm glad we're here for you, but," Mom said, "are we in the way? We could go to the hotel."

Hmmm…that might stop them from drugging me whenever they want.

"That's a good idea. You can go to the hotel once Ted and Kevin leave."

Dad was petting Leonard, who looked at him as if he were his best friend in the world…or a steak with hands. It was hard to tell which. "Okay. I need to make a number of calls for work. I'll let my staff know I'm going to be here awhile."

"I don't want you to upend your life," was what I tried to say, but with a mouthful of pancakes, it came out as "mvxhrthygrth."

"Nonsense," Mom sat down next to me. It didn't surprise me in the least that she understood me. "But we will check into the Radisson if that's what you want. What are your plans for the day?"

"I thought I'd launch a campaign of intimidation and pain until I find my fiancé," I said. Plus I had a poisonous snakey package to track online.

"Well," Dad said. "Don't leave us out of all the fun."

There was a knock at the door, and Leonard barked. He'd started doing that a few weeks ago. As a big Scottish deerhound, he'd suddenly decided that he was protecting us. I was pretty sure he would run away from a menacing butterfly, but the appearance was what was important.

Dad answered the door and returned with Ted and Kevin. To my complete surprise, Officer Dooley wasn't eating. And his uniform wasn't stained with the usual cheese puff dust or powdered sugar.

It felt like I was in an alternate universe.

"Ms. Wrath," Ted said as he shook my hand.

"Please," I insisted. "It's Merry." I shot a look at Kevin to let him know he did not have the same privilege.

"Okay." Ted smiled. "Merry. We've checked out Harvey Oak. He's got a rock-solid alibi. Says he was at a biker rally for the past two days in Boone."

"A biker rally? In January?" I might have sounded a tad sarcastic. "Seems unlikely. I'll bet his biker brothers covered for him."

Ted went on as if I'd said nothing. "And Prescott Winters III claims he was in Winterset for a Covered Bridge Festival."

I shook my head. "That's in the summer." Winterset wasn't far away, and I'd attended the festival last summer with my troop.

"And Vy Todd is unavailable right now." He closed his notepad and looked at me.

"Which means…"

"That we can't find her," Ted Weir answered. "But that doesn't mean she's involved."

I had such high hopes for Officer Weir, but now it seemed that his detection skills were sorely lacking. What did I expect? He was a kid fresh out of the academy. He didn't have the kind of experience that Rex had.

Kevin was openly drooling as he eyed the chocolate chip pancakes. My mother smiled and offered him a plate. I'd never seen someone sit down so fast. Philby waited until he uncovered the bacon then pounced, landing full on the plate. Her victory was short lived. Kevin just shoved her aside, took four strips of bacon, and ate them.

Should I tell them about Juliette Dowd's break-in last...oh wait, two nights ago? I decided not to. She'd just tell them she was at the beach in Des Moines, and these two would believe it. No, I'd keep an eye on her myself.

And I'd go see Riley. He was supposed to see if any of my enemies were in play. It was possible this was an attack from someone who wanted to get back at me. As soon as I could ditch these two and send the folks to the hotel, I'd head over there.

"Good job, guys," I said without a trace of sarcasm. "What's the next move?"

Ted frowned. "I guess I'll run down those alibis."

Kevin looked up at us with a fistful of bacon seasoned with cat hair and shrugged.

The brain trust was obviously on it.

"Sounds good," I said. "I think I'll head over to Ferguson Taxidermy and see if Rex's family has heard anything."

Everyone liked this idea because, presumably, it kept me out of trouble. Little did they know that when it came to Rex, I'd be chasing trouble to the ends of the earth. Ted shook my hand, and after four attempts to get Kevin up from the breakfast bar, the two men left.

"Do you need me to go with you to see the twins?" Mom asked. She'd already cleaned up almost everything.

Philby was glaring at the remaining bacon as if attempting to use the Force to make it fly into his mouth.

Without missing a beat, Mom broke one strip in half and handed each to the cats before throwing the rest in the garbage. Leonard almost had a stroke. I bet I'd be coming home to garbage all over the floor.

"No thanks." I smiled. "I think I've got this."

I needed to do this alone. There was one twin I needed to talk to about handing out keys to my future house to angry redheads who hated me.

# CHAPTER SEVEN

———

"Merry!" Randi dropped the peacock head she'd been carrying and threw her arms around me. "How are you holding up? Isn't this awful?" She released me and patted my arm. "I'm sure Rexley is okay."

Rexley was Rex's real name. He hadn't told me (and made me stop saying it after I spent three days calling him Rexley). The twins had told me about his real name. He wasn't happy about that, nor my idea that we get tattoos with each other's names. What he didn't know was that I had registered everything on our honeymoon, from the hotel to the scuba diving, under Rexley.

I felt a pang of remorse. It seemed wrong making fun of him when he wasn't here to get annoyed. A lingering ache in my gut had been growing since the moment he went missing. Where was he?

"You haven't heard anything?" I wasn't too surprised. Even though we'd used their place as a headquarters, I was pretty sure that with my connections, I'd be the first to find him.

The short, pleasantly plump woman shook her head. "I'm so sorry."

An awkward silence hung heavy in the air between us. Which was really saying something, since right next to me was a remote controlled llama on wheels, who wore a blanket that said *Rex & Merry 4-Ever!* The twins had planned to use it at our reception. It was one of the few taxidermied things I was looking forward to.

I looked around the shop. "Is Ronni here? I need to talk to her about something."

Randi hesitated. "You want to talk to her?" She looked me up and down, no doubt checking for weapons. I wanted to tell her that the dislike was one-sided and I bore Ronni no ill will, but that wasn't exactly accurate since the woman had given Juliette a key to Rex's house and told her I'd kidnapped him.

"Yup," I said. "I ran into someone a couple of days ago in Rex's house. Turns out your twin gave her the key."

There was a flash of dark hair in the doorway. As if Ronni had heard me and jumped back to hide.

The nice twin frowned—for maybe the first time since I'd met her. "Ronni gave someone a key to Rexley's house? I didn't even know we had a key, or I'd have surprised him with something."

She waved to the dioramas that surrounded us.

"Ronni?" she called out.

There was no response, but I saw a clump of dark, unruly hair sticking out of the doorway.

"Ronni? Could you come here please?" She urged in a sugary tone. I'd be willing to bet that Randi cowed her sister with niceties to get her to do stuff.

"I'm busy," came the response from the doorway. "In the basement."

"You are?" Randi asked. "You sound really close."

The voice snapped, "Insanely busy! Trying to finish that order of ring-tailed lemurs for the Norwegians!"

"Oh." Randi sounded disappointed. "Well, if you're too busy…"

I'd had enough of this nonsense.

"You're in the doorway," I called out. "I can actually see you."

The clump of hair vanished. "No, I'm not."

I stomped over there and dragged her into the room where her sister stood, mouth open.

"Did you have a key to Rex's?" Randi asked. She looked worried that I would do something to her twin.

Ronni looked down at the dead stuffed chicken in her arms and started stroking its head. "No."

I was just about to grab two weasels fencing in a duel and use them as a torture device, when Randi looked over her glasses at her sister.

"Ronni?" she asked expectantly.

I waited, armed weasels in hand, to see if she could get her twin to talk.

"Fine!" The petite woman threw her arms up in the air and rolled her eyes. "I made a copy. What's wrong with that?"

"Well," I said evenly. "It's breaking and entering if your brother didn't give you a key."

Ronni glared at the two of us as she started to crush the chicken in her hands. Good thing it was already dead.

"What do you have to say for yourself?" Randi nudged.

It was an unusual dynamic. Randi appeared to be the sweet one and the nurturer. Ronni was the constantly angry one who hated everything and everyone. With the exception of Juliette Dowd, of course.

I couldn't wait. "You gave the key to the woman who might have kidnapped him! I caught her rummaging around in the middle of the night!"

Randi looked worried. Ronni looked murderous.

"Juliette would never hurt Rex! She thinks you did it! I gave her the key to look for clues!"

Her words packed a wallop, and I sat down in the nearest chair—which happened to be a grizzly bear in the seated position with his arms out. He was very comfortable.

"That's outrageous!" Randi shrieked, turning an alarming shade of purple. "Why on earth would Merry kidnap Rex? Have you lost your mind?"

Ronni's face went slack, and I guessed this was the first time her twin had ever blown up on her. The crushed chicken dropped to the floor as she stood there with her mouth open, gawking at Randi.

"I've put up with this long enough!" Randi started pacing. "Juliette is out of the picture! Rex chose Merry!"

I joined Ronni in gaping at Randi.

"If you don't stop acting like this, I'll…I'll…" She looked around and grabbed a wooden meat tenderizer from the table. "You'll get it!"

Ronni seemed to regain her fury, and she scooped up the mangled chicken and ran out of the room.

I arched one eyebrow. "A meat tenderizer?"

Randi took a deep breath and within seconds was back to being sugar and spice. "She's afraid of these." She looked at the tool in her hand. "A kid on the playground, when we were little, brought one down on her foot. I've used this for years to keep her in line. I have one stashed in every room."

She handed it to me, and I took it. Made of solid oak, this would be a formidable weapon. I set down the armed weasels.

"Keep it!" Randi smiled. "I've got a whole gross of them stashed in the attic."

As I walked to my car, it hit me. Juliette was doing the same thing I was. She was looking for Rex too. She was worried about him. For a very brief moment, I toyed with the idea of teaming up with her. And then I regained my senses.

I unlocked my minivan and sat down. Just as I was about to put the key into the ignition, I noticed an envelope on the passenger seat. It was blank. That was odd. I didn't remember it being here earlier. But then, I've been loopy these past few days. It was probably some of the girls' *MISSING* posters. I picked it up and tore it open. Two pieces of paper fell out. One was a blank crossword puzzle with some of the boxes highlighted in yellow.

The second had writing on it:

*Weddings make a family out of two...Let's add in Something New.*

I froze. Very gingerly, I set down the envelope and using a pen, shoved the puzzle and clue aside. Then I called Ted.

\* \* \*

"Was your van locked when you went inside?" Officer Weir held up the clue with gloved hands and squinted at it.

I nodded. "It was. I remember having to unlock it when I came out." I shivered, but not from the cold. "I wasn't even in the shop very long. How could someone break in to my van? I can't find any damage."

Randi and Ronni appeared when the siren came closer. Officer Kevin Dooley pulled into the lot and pulled up next to my van. We stood there, waiting for him to get out, but he didn't. For a second, I thought I saw Ted roll his eyes. Poor guy.

"Officer Dooley." The exasperation was clear in his voice. "Would you join me, please?"

Kevin got out of the car, holding a box of donuts that he did not share with the rest of us.

Ronni scoffed and went back inside, while Randi remained on the porch, wringing her hands.

"The envelope will have my fingerprints on it," I said, ignoring Kevin and talking directly to Ted. "But I didn't touch the other two pieces of paper."

He put them into two separate baggies and ran his hands over the doors of the van.

"This is the same guy," I insisted. "Can I see the crossword again?"

The officer shook his head. "I'm sorry. We need to check it for fingerprints. That's the priority."

"Yes, I get that," I argued. "But we may not have much time to solve this clue."

"I'm really sorry, Merry. I'll get it to you as fast as I can." He set the baggies with the clue and envelope on the hood of the van and asked me to lock and then unlock it. I motioned to Randi on the porch. She came over.

"Do you have a copier?" I whispered.

The woman nodded.

"I think you should bring the nice man a cup of tea."

Randi looked at me and grinned as I slipped her the baggie with the note. Then she disappeared back into the house.

I stepped up to the van. "Try popping the hood," I said. "Maybe they messed with the locking mechanism."

Ted nodded and hit the button inside before walking around and opening the hood. Randi returned momentarily with the note and once I replaced it, offered Officer Weir a cup of tea.

"You know," she offered, "my uncle was a mechanic and taught me all about cars."

He did?

"Why don't I help you take a look?" she asked sweetly.

I shoved the crossword into my pocket as he closed the hood.

"Merry," Ted warned. "I'll get it to you as fast as I can. But I really think we have a good chance of finding fingerprints or DNA. Unfortunately, it's New Year's Eve, so I don't know if anyone will be around."

It was New Year's Eve? "Of course. I can wait." How did I miss that? Oh right, Rex and I were supposed to be celebrating the holiday on a beach.

Officer Dooley started to dust the van for prints. Unfortunately, the powder from the donuts got mixed in with the print powder, and as a result, he found nothing.

"I'm going back inside." I rubbed my arms vigorously. "I'm freezing."

Ted waved me off, and I went back into the shop.

"Here you go." Randi handed me a piece of paper, with one eye on the window.

"Thanks." I unfolded it.

"It's a crossword puzzle." Randi studied it. "I'm terrible at these things."

I smiled. "That's okay, because I know someone who's not."

\* \* \*

One thing that really bothered me as I drove to Linda's condo, was how the kidnapper got into my van. I didn't tell the police this, but I'd installed some extra security a few months ago, which included biometric scanning throughout the exterior of the car.

It had been a pain in the butt when I'd made everyone I know come over and rub their fingers over the van. I'd wanted to make sure my fiancé, best friend, and Girl Scout troop wouldn't be shut out. That, and I didn't want them disabled by the high-pitched squeal the van emitted when it didn't recognize a handprint on the door.

But there'd been no sound. Whoever'd gotten in managed to bypass my security. That pretty much ruled Juliette out. She didn't seem patient or tech savvy enough to avoid detection. So how did the envelope get into my van?

While I'd been doped in my bed for a day, my van had been in my garage. Mom and Dad wouldn't have had any reason to go in there, and the doors had been closed and locked. In fact, I didn't think the envelope had been on the passenger seat when I drove over to Ferguson Taxidermy—Where Your Pet Lives On Forever!

That could only mean that someone got it in there during the ten minutes I was inside the shop. Without tripping the alarm system. Without a key.

A key! Was it someone I knew? Someone who knew about my system and had a copy of my key made? It seemed unlikely, but then again, so was the idea that my big, strong, and smart fiancé could be kidnapped.

I arrived at Linda's with more questions than answers. She met me at the door and led me to her kitchen. If she was surprised when I told her about the break-in, she didn't show it.

"This isn't the original?" she asked as she studied the puzzle.

I shook my head. "It's a copy."

She read aloud, "Weddings make a family of two...Let's add in Something New. The clues seem easy enough," she said. "But it still might take a little while." She pulled a sharp pencil from a drawer and sat down to work.

"What do you think it means...something new?" I asked.

Linda looked up at me. "It's the second line of the poem. The clues are going in order." She shrugged. "Mr. Spitz was old. That's how he tied in to the clue. I'm not sure about *new* though."

"Maybe it's tied to the wedding? We found Leonard Spitz in the first pew on the day of the rehearsal."

The retired teacher thought of this. "The next clue should be about something borrowed. That might have to do with the ceremony. Do you think there's a chance that the next surprise is at the church?"

We called Kelly on the way, and she met us there. The doors were unlocked because the pastor had a meeting. For a moment I stopped to stare at the altar in the rosy, dimming light of a winter afternoon. It really was a pretty church.

My stomach clenched. Someday we were going to get married here. I promised myself it would happen.

"I don't see anything." Kelly came from the front of the church, disrupting my thoughts.

I started walking the aisle, pausing to look under each bench. Linda helped us search the rest of the church. After ten minutes, we called it.

"I guess that would've been too easy." I sighed as we got back into my van. "I'm sorry. I got a little carried away by running off to the church. I should've guessed there were no shortcuts." I just wanted to find Rex. But it looked like this baddie wanted me to stick to his rules.

"The kidnapper doesn't want it to be easy," Linda said. "That's why the puzzle."

My stomach grumbled, and I realized I hadn't had any lunch.

"Why don't we pick up some food at Oleo's," my fourth-grade teacher said. "We'll work better on full stomachs."

"It's New Year's Eve," I said slowly. "If you have plans, I can…" Can what? I didn't have any plans. I guess I could hang out with my parents.

Linda studied me. "I was going to go to a party, but I'd much rather stay in and help you."

I tried not to cry. I really did. This was too much. This nice lady wanted to help me, a kid she hadn't seen in years. I looked over at Kelly as the tears ran down my face.

She shook her head. "I don't have anything better to do either. Robert's sister and her family are visiting. They will have a great time with Finn. I'll stay with you."

How did I end up with such great friends? I wiped the tears away and nodded. Kelly understood.

Twenty minutes later, after dodging many drunken revelers at the restaurant, we were back at the condo. It started to snow outside as darkness fell. Linda set the table in the kitchen, and Kelly and I opened the cartons. Kelly and Linda had salads. I had the biggest burger they had—the Artery Clogger 2000. Meat always made me feel better.

As we ate, we took turns looking at the crossword. It looked like a normal puzzle to me. Riley and I worked on them a lot when on surveillance. But some of the boxes were highlighted in this puzzle. I'd never seen that before. Solving the crossword wouldn't be enough. Linda would have a word scramble to deal with once she was finished.

"These are such short clues," Kelly said, frustrated. "How can you get an answer out of 'egg'?"

Our former teacher nodded. "That's the trick. And often the answer isn't what you think it is." She picked up her pencil. "For example, it could mean the way the egg is cooked, like fried, over easy, or poached. Or it's referring to the animal who lays it. Or it's a reference to human reproduction."

"One word could mean all that?" Kelly asked.

She nodded. "And then there are synonyms, antonyms…thousands of other options. So you look at how many letters you need. In this case, it's three. So I'm going to say 'roe.'"

"Fish eggs?" I asked.

"That's the only thing I can think of that has three letters. It could be 'eat,' or 'fry,' but I think that's a bit of a reach. Now I could be wrong, but we have to finish the puzzle to find out. When you find a word you know is the right answer, then you can judge connecting words."

Kelly and I ate and watched in awe as Linda Willard started to fill in the blanks. On a pad of paper, she kept a running list of other possible answers to the clues. Every rare now and then, she'd erase an answer and try another word. She was right. This was going to take a while.

We cleared the table. I even took out the trash, stomping through an inch of the powder. I lingered in the doorway on my way back. It was so pretty when it snowed at night. Rex and I would go out on his covered deck and curl up on a wicker sofa and watch it all come down.

I missed him. And I was sure he missed me. I knew he was counting on me to find him. Rex wasn't the kind of guy who needed to be macho all the time. He was okay with my particular skill set—unless I used it to get in his way. Right now, I'd do anything to have him lecture me on interfering with his investigations.

"Merry." Kelly frowned as she handed me the phone I'd left in the kitchen. "You got a message that the rattlesnake you ordered was denied because you didn't submit proof that you're a herpetologist?"

I snatched the phone. "Oh! That! I was, um, doing some research."

She folded her arms over her chest. "You tried to order a poisonous snake, for research?"

"Well, yes. Of course. Why?" Always throw it back in their laps if you can't think of a good reason for doing something…like trying to buy a venomous snake.

Kelly wasn't buying it. For a moment, I thought I was going to get a lecture, but then she relaxed and took out her phone. She was talking to Robert in seconds and chatting about things.

Meanwhile, I was trying to figure out how I was going to break in to the zoo to milk a snake. I've never done it, but I once saw a guy in Marrakesh milk an ostrich. Of course, if I go to the zoo, I have to see Mr. Fancy Pants, my adopted king vulture. In a way, he was my therapist. Unofficially of course, for the reason that he can't give advice other than a vulturish glare.

Then there was the small fact that the Obladi Zoo is closed for the season, and because of a lion attack in July, they've stepped up security. I used to have a key to the aviary. Okay, I had a stolen key. I visited all the time, taking the vulture Girl Scout Cookies.

Sadly, I didn't have any, and if I did, sneaking off to the zoo would take time away from the investigation. And Susan, my human therapist, was out of town for the holidays.

"Do you want any champagne?" Kelly appeared at my side. "Linda doesn't have any on hand, but I could run home."

I shook my head. "No. I need to keep a clear head from here on out."

Before I knew what was happening, my best friend crushed me in a bear hug. "I'm sorry this is happening, Merry," she said when she released me. "We will find him. I know we will. And next New Year's Eve we will have a huge party to make up for this."

"Next year, I'll be celebrating my one-year anniversary," I mused.

She put an arm around me. "You will. You'll be an old married woman by this time next year." For some odd reason, this made Kelly giggle. The giggles gave way to outright laughter. I was pretty sure I didn't want to know why.

Instead, I wandered back into the kitchen where Linda was about a third of the way through the puzzle. She was really good. I remembered a day in her class when she taught us how to do word-find puzzles, where you circle the word on a graph of letters.

Those were my favorite puzzles. The teacher kept a box of pages on her desk, and if you finished an assignment early, you could take one and solve it. Linda didn't believe in idle time in a classroom. She thought you should work the whole time you were there. But she didn't say it couldn't be fun.

My nerves were on edge, and I felt cagey, pacing throughout the kitchen as she worked. If I annoyed her, she didn't say anything. After an hour, Linda stood up and stretched. That was when I noticed it was getting late and she was getting tired. Part of me wanted to make her work until done. But I just couldn't do it. We needed her sharp.

"We should head out," I said slowly, waiting for her to stop me.

She didn't.

"We still have empty boxes in the puzzle," Linda said. "Some are filled with mostly vowels. Which means we're getting there."

"Are those numbers?" I asked as I looked over her shoulder.

"I think so, but I'm not sure. This is supposed to be a challenge. The bad guy doesn't want it to be easy. In the end, we may have to unscramble what's in the highlighted boxes."

"I can't thank you enough." My eyes were going a bit misty.

Linda patted my shoulder and looked me in the eyes, "It's going to be alright, Merry. You'll see. I'll call you in the morning."

As we said our good-byes and Kelly and I drove our separate ways, I wondered who would use this kind of method to torment me? But I was tired, and my brain was begging me to sleep, so I eased into the driveway and went inside.

My parents, as they'd promised, weren't there. They'd left a note saying they'd taken Leonard out and fed all of the animals. That was good, because it was one less thing for me to do. Philby tried to trick me into feeding her again by staring a hole through my head. She was very talented at angry, persuasive staring, and I gave up a can of tuna. Which caused Leonard to give me the begging eyes.

Dogs and cats have very different attitudes on manipulation. While Leonard tried to look sad and dejected, Philby used intimidation. Was that normal, or was it just my pets? I wondered. I unwrapped a cheese stick, and he swallowed it without chewing.

Getting ready for bed was a chore. It was hard to get undressed. If Rex turned up or someone wearing a sign that said he'd kidnapped my fiancé turned up outside my door, I wanted to be ready to go. So, I sat on my bed, fully dressed, and thought about what had happened today.

Someone broke into my van. A vehicle that I'd made very hard to break into. That nagged at me because it seemed like something a spy could do. I knew Linda would solve the crossword, but I wasn't too sure about Ted Weir. He'd shown promise at first, but it seemed to me that he'd dropped the ball on the ex-cons. Maybe I should cut him some slack. He's very young and new at this. And I needed all the help I could get.

Was it Harvey Oak? Prescott Winters III? Vy Todd? Had someone from Rex's past decided to take their revenge?

Or was it someone who was out to get me? If so, that was going to be a very long list. And I knew how to winnow it down. I texted Riley and told him to be at his office early in the morning.

We had a list of our own to investigate.

# CHAPTER EIGHT

———

As I walked through the door in the morning, I noticed that my former handler had been busy. New furniture filled the room of his strip mall office. Two desks sat at opposite ends of the room, which seemed optimistic on his part since I'd turned down his offer of a job.

In the middle of the room were two overstuffed leather love seats, facing each other. On the ends were two leather wingback chairs. In the middle was a long, rectangular coffee table. Riley had obviously been shopping at Midland Furniture, the town's only furniture store. It was currently under new management after a rather disastrous turn of events back in October.

"Give me a minute." Riley held one finger up without taking his eyes off his computer monitor.

I nodded and sat on the sofa. That was when I noticed the gorgeous green plants and beautiful artwork on the walls. He'd really gone to a lot of trouble.

And then it hit me. Where did he live? He'd been here, setting up his private investigation business for a few months now. He couldn't be staying at the Radisson, could he? No, Mom and Dad would've said if they'd seen him there. But if he had a house, why didn't I know that?

Maybe because I didn't want to know. Riley had the bad habit of popping in and out of my life, sometimes to help me, and sometimes to drive me crazy. I'd kept him at arm's length, so it seemed legit that I'd made no effort to find out where he was staying.

I shouldn't be that way. We had a past. And we'd worked very well together. Sure, we'd had a brief romantic fling, but we'd been partners for years. And Kelly (who had Riley's number on speed dial) had told me that he was happy for me and Rex. I was being a selfish friend for not showing more interest in his life.

"Okay." Riley sat on the opposite couch and set a couple of file folders on the coffee table.

"Before we start," I said. "Where do you live?"

Riley arched his right eyebrow. "You don't know?"

I didn't have time for this. "No. I just wondered. I've been a little distracted this past year. Where are you staying?"

He wanted to tease me—I could see it in his eyes. But in the end, he didn't.

"I have a nice house at the opposite end of town from you. It's small, more like a bungalow. It'll make an amazing bachelor pad." He grinned, white teeth gleaming against impossibly bronze skin.

"Okay, I don't care anymore," I said tiredly. "What have you got?"

Riley laughed. "I've talked to a couple of contacts, and there's a lot going on since I retired."

"Going on? What does that mean?" I was getting a little irritated with his usual theatrics.

He leaned back against the sofa. "There have been some developments in a few cases you've worked on. Bad developments."

I shrugged. "That's just the life of a spy. What's happened?"

For a moment I thought he wasn't going to tell me. Surely he knew me better than that. I once threw him through a plate glass window for teasing me. Okay, it was on the first floor, it was safety glass, and he'd landed in some nice, soft bushes, but still…

"I'll cut right to the chase." He opened the file, rotating it toward me, and the photos of two women made me jump.

*No!*

"Lana was traded to Russia in a spy swap a month ago," he started. "And Leiko Ito has escaped from a maximum security prison."

"You're joking," I said weakly as I picked up the two photos.

Lana, or Svetlana Babikova, had been a Russian agent I'd turned years ago. After I'd made my rather involuntary exit from the CIA, the agency hustled her out of Ukraine and brought her here for safekeeping.

In fact, Riley had brought the buxom bimbo to my house, thinking it was the safest place for her to hide out. But he'd been wrong. It hadn't been the safest place for anyone after her arrival. Needless to say, she was serving time in prison. Or so I'd thought.

Leiko Ito was the daughter of Midori—a ruthless Yakuza lady boss who, on more than one occasion, had tried to kill me. Naturally, the evil mob boss turned up dead in my house. And Leiko came after me and Riley for revenge. She had also been sent to a hardcore prison. A prison she'd managed to escape from. The Yakuza have a long reach.

"They must've skipped out of the country," I insisted. "Leiko is back in Tokyo, and Lana is probably rotting in a Siberian jail."

Riley shrugged. "We don't know. Both of them have disappeared. Gone underground. There's zero chatter about them anywhere. It's like they vanished into thin air."

"That's possible," I said slowly, staring at Lana's huge blue eyes and impossibly glossy blonde hair. "The Russians could've killed her for turning on them and hiding out here. Do we know what she thought of the exchange?"

He pulled a sheet from the file and read it. "According to her cell mate, Lana was thrilled about the exchange."

I frowned. "That doesn't make any sense." Nothing did.

"And Leiko? How did she break out?"

"The Yakuza got to the guards. Threatened three of them, which got them to cooperate. In fact, the reason we still don't know how she escaped is because these three men are too terrified to talk."

I slumped against the back of the couch and closed my eyes. It just wasn't fair. Here I was, ready to get married and start a new life, and now people I'd helped lock up were on the loose.

"My spy skills are getting too rusty to handle this," I groaned.

I wasn't fit for duty. Sure, I could still break in to places, and my fighting form wasn't that bad, but I'd been out of the game for three years. That's like four decades when you consider the constant changes in technology.

"It might not be them," Riley said. "Like you said, Lana is probably languishing in a Russian prison, and Leiko went back to Tokyo to get a grip on her vast Japanese enterprise." He picked up another sheet. "It looks like her businesses are failing at a rapid pace. She'd need to get home and straighten things out."

I buried my face in my hands. "This can *not* be happening."

Ex-cons, I was fairly certain, I could handle. A chop shop thief, a one-time murderer, and a drug smuggler? No problem. But two lethally trained harpies with a thirst for vengeance and some killer skills? I wasn't so sure.

After a moment, I sat up and took a deep breath. There was no time to panic.

"We need to know if there's anyone new in town—someone who seems out of place."

Riley agreed. "I'll check with the Radisson and the two other hotels in the area. Maybe my Fed buddies can scout the hotels in Des Moines."

I shook my head. "If they're in the city, they're at a safe house. Here, they'd be in a hotel."

"You say that like you think they are working together," Riley said.

"I hope that's not true. But we have to be prepared."

Riley studied the files, "If Leiko is here, she'd have a couple of her lieutenants with her. Shouldn't be too hard to find a small Japanese woman flanked by two or three giant Japanese men."

"And if it's Lana?" I asked.

He blew out a sharp breath and leaned back. "We might be screwed. She lived here. She knows where you live, where Kelly lives, and who's in your troop. One woman is much harder to track than three or four Yakuza."

Riley was right. Lana knew a lot about me.

"I'll move the animals to Rex's house and set up some major security measures." I thought for a moment. I'd need a pet sitter. Maybe Kelly knew someone.

"I'll get back to you once I've asked at the hotels." Riley closed the file with a snap. "Where will you be staying?"

"In my house. I know it better and have all my weaponry there." I ran through a mental inventory in my head. Guns, check. Knives, check. Flamethrower made from an Altoids tin, check.

He stood up and frowned. "I don't think that's a good idea."

I shrugged. "We have clues coming in. To me. I need to be where I can find them."

It was time to brief him. I told Riley about the clues, the three ex-convicts who might be suspects, Linda, and Juliette Dowd's break-in at Rex's house. He listened patiently and waited to speak until I was done.

"Rex was the one who arrested Vy Todd?" Riley gaped. "Wow. That was a huge deal."

"How did you know about her?" I asked.

Riley shrugged, "She's actually my second cousin."

"What?" I screamed. "How did I not know that? You were in Mongolia with me when we found out! You didn't say anything about it then!"

"I guess I didn't think it mattered. I'd only met her once or twice at family reunions. It's not like I *knew* her."

"You're related to her!" I shrieked. "We actually talked about this case when we were in that yurt!"

He grinned. "That's not all we did in that yurt."

I threw the only thing I had on hand, a pillow, at his head. He ducked.

"Okay," he protested. "I should've told you."

"You knew I was from Iowa!" I wasn't letting this go.

"I'm sorry," he said.

Not sorry enough. "You have some lovely floor-to-ceiling windows here," I mused.

Riley blanched, but only for a second. "I'll see if anyone in the family has seen her since she moved to Des Moines. It's a long shot, but maybe I can find something there."

"What am I supposed to do? You're doing all the legwork!" I whined. "I don't want to sit home and wait for Lana or Leiko to attack."

"I'd love to tell you that they're probably not involved, but…" His voice trailed off.

I narrowed my eyes. "But what?"

"Broke into your van without leaving a trace?" Riley whistled. "That's pretty sophisticated for your average criminal. Because I suspect you have some special security measures, like I do. And if you can't figure out how they got in…"

I stood, grabbed his arm, and dragged him out to the van. Unlocking the vehicle, I reached in and pulled out two flashlights, handing one to Riley. This was one thing I could do right now. He nodded and took the driver's side, while I took the passenger side.

We'd had training in looking for car bombs and that sort of thing. In the back of my mind, I wondered if we were chasing phantoms. Were we too eager to believe this had something to do with my past? It still could be someone local. My head was spinning with the possibilities, and I was angry that I wasn't any closer to solving this.

I needed something to do, and it didn't matter if it was busy work. Either this was a spy from my past or someone from my present. We might as well search the van. I started with the front passenger door, going over the mechanics with the flashlight. I'd installed a small alarm that would go off if the door was opened with something other than the factory-issued key. Tiny wires ran from the edge of the doorframe to the mechanism. They were intact. If someone had jimmied open the door, the wires would've been cut and the alarm would've sounded.

Next, I focused on the window. Turning the key in the ignition, I hit the controls that made the window move up and down. I'd installed a sort of gummy substance, whose chemical compound is classified, to make the windows stick just a bit before working. If the windows operated smoothly, the gummy substance was gone, and I'd know that someone came in that way. Nope. The windows stuck a bit. And I tried all four.

Inside the van, I ran the flashlight over every bit of leather on the door. There was a chance that someone got past my security and tore open the upholstery. The seams were all intact, and there were no holes.

I repeated this procedure on the other door, with the same results. Riley reported the same. We popped the hood on the car and together went over every single centimeter of the engine and other mechanics. This was where I was less qualified, but Riley assured me that nothing was out of place.

The snow on the ground was frozen hard, but that didn't stop us from lying down and studying the undercarriage. I was pretty sure they couldn't get into the van this way, but you have to check everything, no matter how tedious. Skipping steps makes for dead spies.

"The trunk?" Riley asked over the top of the van when we stood back up.

I nodded. This was a definite possibility because my security measures were lacking there. I remembered the day I worked in the garage to set things up. At one point, I was hungry and wandered into the house for some Pizza Rolls. I was pretty sure from there I got dessert, some wine, and never made it back out to the garage.

Under the gloomy, gray sky, Riley and I went over the tailgate.

"The thing is," I mumbled. "Going through the back of the van was a risk. Once inside, you'd have to climb over seats and reach over the headrest to place the clue."

Riley nodded. "It would definitely take more time. Probably would've added to the intruder's time to get in and out."

"I was inside the house for a while." I sighed. "How much time he took might not have mattered."

Nonetheless, we continued going over every inch of the back door. And we came up with nothing.

"Come on," Riley said. "I can make some hot tea."

Once we started warming up, Riley made a couple of calls to his family. I tuned him out. He'd brief me if he found something. I wondered if Linda was working on the puzzle. It was almost eleven, and I'd bet she was.

My stomach rumbled.

"Well," Riley joined me. "I've called a few relatives. No one has been in contact with Vy since she went to prison."

"Do you believe them?"

Riley frowned. "I do. None of them are in the espionage business. But I'll follow up. They don't live in Iowa, so if she's in Des Moines, it would make sense she'd go underground."

My stomach roared.

I got up and grabbed my coat. "Tell you what. It's time for lunch, and I hear the Radisson has a mean stuffed pork chop. Let's go. After, you can investigate and I'll run by Linda's to see how far she is on the clue. Deal?"

"Deal."

* * *

I texted Mom before I left Riley's, inviting them to lunch. It would be bad manners not to. Riley met me there five minutes later and held the door open for me as we walked in.

The Flying Pig, the restaurant in the hotel, was part of a chain throughout the state. I'd never eaten at this one, but I knew of their reputation for an authentic, stuffed Iowa chop. The name also appealed to me. Although, so did the irony that if pigs could fly, this place wouldn't be able to make a mean pork chop.

Mom and Dad waved us over to a table, and we joined them. The décor was simple, with barn doors, wood walls, and a few plaster pigs with wings suspended from the ceiling. But the scent of fried, grilled, and smoked meat turned me into a drooling, monosyllabic carnivore. The waitress took our orders then dropped off a bowl of steaming homemade rolls and a cup of honey butter. I dug in.

"So, Riley." My dad buttered a roll, but I was on my second already. "How's the new business?"

Mom put her hand on my arm, a gesture she has always used on me when she didn't want me to fill up on bread and save room for dinner. Here, she was probably making sure I'd fit into my wedding dress when the wedding did take place. I finished the second roll and set my knife down on my plate.

"It's coming along, Senator." Riley hadn't touched his bread. He was averse to carbs or anything unhealthy. "It takes time, but since I'm technically retired, I'm not in a rush."

"This is your first case then?" Mom asked. She was just now buttering a roll. It would be her only one.

He grinned. "I guess so."

"It's pro bono," I said quickly. There was no way that Riley was getting one penny from me.

"Okay." Riley laughed. "But I get bragging rights."

Bragging rights. Rex was missing, and Riley wanted bragging rights when we found him. Fine. He could have that. After all, I'd get Rex. That was the big prize.

Mom sensed what I was thinking. "I postponed the wedding with the church, caterer, and reception. And I cancelled the honeymoon reservations. This is just a setback, that's all." She smiled and squeezed my hand.

"And I'm taking vacation time," Dad said, squeezing my other hand.

Riley rubbed my foot with his, possibly because he felt left out. I kicked him. Hard.

"Riley's not the only one helping," I said as I went ahead and buttered a third roll. "Do you guys remember my fourth-grade teacher? Linda?"

Dad nodded. "I'd heard she retired. The teachers lost a real champion when she left."

"What about her?" Mom asked as the waitress set down our drinks.

I explained about the puzzle I'd found. "And she's kind of a puzzle master. She's working on it right now."

"Who are the suspects?" Dad asked.

Riley explained about the three criminals that Rex had put away. He *forgot* to mention that he was related to Vy Todd.

"Vy Todd? Really? Good Lord!" Dad started.

"We know Prescott Winters II," Mom offered.

Riley gaped, "You know the man who killed his wife?"

She shook her head. "No, his father. He was a major donor to your dad's campaign until that strange heart attack."

Dad nodded. "His son was a bad sort. When his mother died a month later, also from a heart attack, he inherited and cut the ties to all of his parents' legacy charities. A couple of the nonprofits folded under the strain of their budgets. It was too bad."

"His parents would've been horrified," Mom added. "They were very generous people. It would've broken their hearts."

I leaned forward. "They all died of heart attacks? Sounds suspicious."

"One investigation at a time." Mom patted my hand.

"And Prescott III's wife? How did she die?" I had to ask.

"Her parents were even wealthier than his. Only child and orphaned. Fell down a flight of stairs," Dad said. "The detective at the time noticed that there was way too much blood at the bottom of the stairs for it to be a simple accident."

"That was Rex," I explained. "Rex was the detective for that case too."

It was so good to hear this story. My heart swelled as I thought of him making the arrest of this greedy kid. Why hadn't I asked Rex about his life before I'd met him? How selfish of me to never ask questions about his past cases.

I was learning so much now. It didn't seem fair that he wasn't here to be amused by my interest. When I got him back, I was going to make it up to him. And I would have to grill him for more stories.

"What about Harvey Oak?" Riley asked. "He was local. Is that a family name around here?"

I hadn't thought of that.

Mom looked at Dad. "I think there were one or two around here at one time."

Dad shrugged. "I'm sorry, but I don't know."

The food arrived, along with food for thought. We had five suspects. They were weak suspects, but I needed to have someone in my mind, even though it was possible that it was someone else. I'd love for it to be Juliette Dowd. A flash of fury coursed in my veins as I remembered catching her in Rex's house, but that didn't mean she wasn't keeping Rex in her basement. There was a break-in in my near future.

No one discussed the case while we were eating. You have to enjoy an Iowa stuffed chop in reverent silence. Thick, juicy, and filled up with apple glazed stuffing, there's nothing like it in the world. The closest I ever came across was in Nicaragua, but that had been a badly burned bit of pig flesh on a stick coated in a paste made of dead ants. Not the same. At all.

We were just looking over the dessert menu (yes, I was still hungry) when I got a call from Linda Willard.

"Mom, Dad," I said as I stood and slipped on my coat. "I've got to go. But Riley's picking up the check, so don't fight him on that." I slid a look at Riley, whose face remained unruffled.

I grabbed a roll, buttered it, and took it with me. What? In my line of work, you never know when you'll eat next.

Linda met me at the door. I don't know how she knew when I'd be there.

"You solved it?" I asked as I followed her into the kitchen.

"Almost," she said. "I'm close, but there are a couple of answers missing. Since I believe this is about you, I thought you might be able to help."

The puzzle was mostly filled in. All but three of the highlighted boxes now had letters in them. The margins of the puzzle were filled with words, some crossed out.

She pointed to a string of letters on the bottom. "This is what I have so far."

There were a lot of letters in random order across the bottom and a few numbers spelled out.

"What are the ones you can't figure out?"

Linda handed me the puzzle, and we sat down at the table. "I marked them for you. Would you like some hot cocoa?"

I nodded eagerly since I didn't get dessert. Dessert is very important.

Three prompts stared back at me. Might as well get this over with. The first one said, *Tolstoy*. That was easy. There were seven blanks. *Ice pick*. Leonid Tolstoy was killed in Mexico by an ice pick. That might not be the right answer, but if it was aimed at me, this was what a spy would think of.

The second prompt was *Moscow*. Hmmm...trickier. Could they be referring to the *Moscow Rules*? There were ten of those. Written during the Cold War for spies in the Soviet Union, they were ten things to remember when working in Moscow. Based on common sense, if you followed these rules, you might avoid capture. I had them memorized, like the spies of old did, because they were cool and good common sense:

1) Assume nothing.
2) Never go against your gut.
3) Everyone is potentially under opposition control.
4) Do not look back; you are never completely alone.
5) Go with the flow, blend in.
6) Vary your pattern and stay within your cover.
7) Lull them into a sense of complacency.
8) Do not harass the opposition.
9) Pick the time and place for action.
10) Keep your options open.

I counted the number of squares and found thirteen. There was only one that was that short, *Assume nothing*. I carefully plugged in those letters. That gave us two more highlighted squares. These were certainly spy related, which made me think Lana and Leiko, who knew me as a former spy, were behind this.

There was only one more prompt: Marco. I froze. Forcing myself to count the open squares made my lungs constrict.

"That one really stumped me," Linda said as she joined me. "With five letters, you'd think it would be Polo, right? But that's only four letters."

One clue intersected, but I knew what that letter was before I looked at it.

*No. It can't be.*

"Are you okay, Merry?" Linda looked alarmed.

The answer to that question was no. I knew the solution, but I was afraid to put it down.

"It's *manic*," I whispered.

Seeing that I'd been rendered useless, Linda gently took the puzzle from me and filled it in.

My old teacher sat down and with a new piece of paper, wrote out all the highlighted letters, and went to work.

I could barely breathe. Marco Manic. It was a code name for a very classified mission. The only one I ever failed. It was even before Riley's time, so he wouldn't know it.

Marco Manic was the one case where I'd lost my contact.

This was definitely about me.

# CHAPTER NINE

My second mission with the CIA took place in Istanbul. My handler was a man we'll call Frank. He was retiring after this mission and had already phoned it in. I got no guidance from him. He spent all of his time drinking in whatever dive bar was closest.

But I was young and an idiot and thought I could do this myself. After all, it was a simple case. I had to turn an assistant to the assistant of the deputy prime minister. No problem.

The guy's name was Marco. Well, that was the name we assigned him. He was young, fresh out of college, and eager. Turning him wasn't that hard. He felt that Turkey was heading down the wrong path, and I'd convinced him that if he stole one or two files, we could change things for the better.

The lies we tell...

Because I was young and stupid, I gave reckless advice. Marco was discovered floating in the river, a bullet hole in his head. I found Frank in a cheap bar, sobered him up, and got him out of the country.

He was immediately retired and got his full pension. The last I'd heard, he still hung out in bars, just better ones

I got sent back to the Farm for more training. Marco got a shameful burial in a pauper's grave. I never forgot it.

"How long has she been like this?" I heard Kelly whisper.

"Two hours," Linda replied. "Do you know what's wrong?"

I felt a hard thump on my back between my shoulder blades. It shook me out of my dreamlike trance.

"Did you just Heimlich me?" I asked my best friend.

Kelly nodded. "She's back. And for your information, the Heimlich maneuver is totally different."

"Oh good." Linda smiled. "Because I've solved the puzzle."

"What is it?" I was a little shaken from my trip down bad memory lane.

"It's an address." Kelly frowned.

"Let's go," I said as I raced out the door. I ran back in because I'd forgotten my keys, coat, and purse. I collected the two women and the clue and got into the van.

"1221 Titmouse Street," Kelly read from the backseat as I drove like a maniac.

Someone was likely dead at this address. But maybe, just maybe, they'd be alive. It wouldn't be Rex. Linda had convinced me that we had two more clues coming. But someone was there. *Someone new.*

My mind raced as I considered the possibilities. But my mind was so jumbled I could barely focus on driving.

"There it is!" Kelly pointed over my shoulder.

It was four thirty, so it would be dark very soon. I took the flashlights out of the car and handed them to the other women. Then I turned on my cell's flashlight.

The address was that of a small craftsman cottage. It was small and sweet and had a lot more character than my little ranch house. And now, like my house had had many times in the past, there was probably a dead body somewhere on the grounds.

"Should we go in?" Kelly asked.

"Ladies?" Linda said from my right. "I can see something through the window. There's someone sleeping on the couch."

That was all she needed to say. I raced up to the door and beat on it with my fists. Then I looked at Linda.

She shook her head. "No movement at all."

I slipped on my gloves and turned the knob. To my surprise, it was unlocked. The three of us stepped into an elegant art deco hallway with hand-crafted hardwood floors. Ignoring the plastic boot tray – placed there so visitors or thoughtful killers wouldn't track snow inside - we made our way to the room where Linda had seen the body.

Sitting up and sightless, on a beautiful, brown velvet couch, was a young man I'd never seen before. Ligature marks ringed his neck, but there was no murder weapon present. I stepped forward to study him, and Kelly called 9-1-1.

The man was young, maybe twenty-five. He had short brown hair and brown eyes. I closed them. Yes, I know you aren't supposed to do that, but I couldn't have him staring at me like that, could I?

The victim was dressed in a dark gray three-piece suit and a royal blue tie. It looked tailored. His shoes were more than one year's salary for me. I was pretty sure they were custom made.

"Who is he?" Kelly asked.

I shook my head. "No idea. You don't recognize him?"

Both women shook their heads.

Sirens wailed in the distance.

That woke me up. "We have to look around the room, take in everything. There's not much time."

The three of us wandered around, noting anything we could. The room was a study, and it was immaculate. Was this the victim's home? He must've been new to town. That was why the *new* clue.

But who was he, and why was he killed?

The door burst open, and Officer Weir, accompanied by Dr. Body, walked into the room. Ted took several pictures with his cell phone and then nodded to Soo Jin, who carefully examined the deceased.

"Do you know him?" he asked.

I shook my head. "None of us do. But he was our clue."

The man looked confused, so Linda took him aside and patiently explained, like a good teacher did, what happened to bring us here. I was waiting for a lecture on how I should've called the police first, but to be fair, none of us really knew what we'd find.

"Ms. Wrath?" Officer Weir spoke up. "I understand that this is personal, but please include me when you get the next clue. I can help." His voice was pleading, and I kind of felt bad.

Soo Jin held out a wallet. Ted put on gloves and opened it.

"Marco Jones. Says he's from Virginia."

Marco? Alarm bells sounded in my head. Maybe this was just a coincidence.

"What's going on?" Riley was standing in the hallway, looking in at us. He must've seen my car and stopped.

"The clue told us to come here," I said.

Riley looked at the man on the couch, and he slumped against the wall, his face in his hands. I walked over to him.

"You know this man."

He nodded. "I know this man."

"And his name is Marco?" I asked.

Riley shook his head. "That's one of his covers. His name is Bobby Ray Pratt. He was your replacement at Langley."

"He's CIA?" I asked weakly.

"He is." Riley glanced at the corpse. "Was."

"How did you know to find us here?" Kelly asked. "Did you follow us?"

Riley responded, "No. I found you because"—he took a deep breath—"this is my house."

# CHAPTER TEN

———

"So this really is about me," I mumbled for the third time.

Kelly introduced Linda Willard around to everyone and then explained to her that I'd been a spy. The woman listened carefully then nodded. Kelly had forgotten that she'd followed my situation in the papers and knew I was ex-CIA. But because she was a classy lady, Linda never corrected her.

"That's why this fits," she said. "Something new. Mr. Pratt was your replacement, so he's new. As in, Something New."

"I'm going to remove the body," Soo Jin told Ted. "Is there anything else you need?"

The officer shook his head. He looked confused and frustrated. I felt a little sorry for him. He wasn't a detective and was in way over his head.

"Sheriff Carnack had given me permission to investigate, but I think I'm stepping on your toes here."

Ted shook his head. "You aren't. I'm pretty new here. You have far more knowledge and experience."

"Thanks." I felt a little better.

"But." Isn't there always a *but*? "We are all running around here like chickens with our heads cut off. We need to communicate and work together."

I appreciated the Iowa metaphor. "What's your role at the station?"

He looked sheepish. "I'm kind of taking the lead, what with Detective Ferguson gone, with approval from the sheriff. I hope that's okay."

I thought about the small police station. There were just three uniforms: this guy, Kevin, and Rex. Most of them just wanted to do their jobs and go home. We often got forensics backup from Des Moines or the Iowa State Police.

"It's totally okay," I reassured him. "Besides, you've got access to all kinds of resources that I can't use otherwise."

The young man brightened. "I'll help any way I can. I like it here, but someday I'd like to be in the FBI." He ran off to give orders to Kevin.

Riley joined me, and we watched as orderlies from the hospital bagged the body and lifted it onto a cart. Something fluttered as they lifted him. I snagged a pair of gloves out of one of the orderly's pockets (he didn't notice) and picked it up.

"Another crossword puzzle?" Riley said over my shoulder.

Linda and Kelly raced over. He was right. That was exactly what it was. Just like the other one, some of the blank boxes were highlighted.

"Where's the poem?" Linda frowned. "There should be a poem about Something Borrowed."

We poked around to see if we could find anything else. Panic flared in my chest as I got down on my knees to peer under the couch. What if we didn't have the whole clue? A part of the wedding poem came with each puzzle—except for this time. Did that mean we wouldn't be able to solve it and move forward?

"Maybe it's in the crossword this time?" Kelly suggested. "Before we freak out, we should see if that's the case."

"Do you have a copier?" I asked.

Riley nodded, and I followed him to a sumptuous home office.

"Wow." I stared at the bookshelves loaded with books. "You're a reader?"

He ignored me as he lifted the lid, and I dropped the sheet onto the machine. Seconds later, we had a copy, and I found Ted Weir and turned the original over to him.

"Thanks," he said as he put it in a plastic bag. "I haven't heard back from the lab on the first one yet. Probably because of the holiday. I'll send this over right away. Sheriff Carnack and I are meeting tomorrow morning for a briefing. He seems to have faith in me."

If the sheriff trusted him, it was time I did. I stopped him. "Sorry I made a copy of the first one and didn't tell you."

His frustration melted into a weak smile. "Hey, you figured it out, which saved us time. I'm sure you made a copy of this one too, right?" He didn't wait for me to answer. "Just promise me you'll let me know before you run off to the next clue."

I agreed.

A forensics team showed up a few moments later and began to dust the furniture where the body had been. Riley invited us into a dining room with upholstered chairs and a large teak table.

"How can you afford all this?" I asked.

CIA and FBI agents didn't make a lot of money. And unless he had a rich relative who died recently and left him a huge inheritance, his expensive digs looked suspicious.

"I had an uncle who died recently and left me a huge inheritance." He shrugged.

We all sat down, and Riley disappeared into what I assumed was the kitchen. He returned with bottles of sparkling water and a platter filled with fruit and cheese. Kevin stuck his head in—probably sensing food. But Ted shouted, and he vanished.

Linda pulled a pencil from her purse and started working on the puzzle.

"I like your house," Kelly said.

Riley thanked her and sat down at the head of the table. "I fell in love with it the minute I saw it."

"There's an anagram in the clues. Tiny tick marks beside certain letters. I think there are two clues here," Linda announced, and we crowded around her.

Kelly sighed. "That's a lot of letters. This will take a while."

Linda smiled. "Not necessarily. We already know three words that have been in both of the other clues...*Let's, something, and borrowed.*" She cast a sympathetic eye in my direction. "I'm sure it's part of this puzzle. The kidnapper is just changing things up. So we plug in those words and…"

"You just have to eliminate those letters…" I finished.

"…and use the ones you have left!" Riley finished. "Linda, you should've been a spy."

She smiled at him. "What I did was much more difficult, but thank you anyway."

I suppressed a chuckle. She was right. She had Kevin Dooley as a student, and I'm sure there were many more over the years. Linda would've made a great spy with that kind of experience.

She got to work, so Riley gave Kelly and me a tour. For a small cottage, this was larger than it looked. And so well decorated, it looked like something out of a magazine. How did he do it? My house, the very first place I owned, had a couch, TV, bed, and *Dora the Explorer* sheets for drapes. For over a year.

"It really is lovely, Riley," Kelly said.

"Thanks." He had the good grace to blush. "I did it myself."

We were interrupted by one of the forensics guys, who said they were leaving and that we could clean up. It wasn't too bad. Just dust everywhere. Kelly ran for supplies as I asked a few questions.

"Did you find any fingerprints?"

The man nodded. "Three. I'll send the report to Officer Weir. Good night."

I turned to Riley. "Where was Bobby Ray from?"

"West Virginia, I think. A tiny town. His parents were farmers."

"Wealthy farmers?"

He shook his head. "Not at all. He said he came from the wrong side of the tracks."

"So why the bespoke three-piece suit and expensive shoes?" I asked. "With that background and the crappy government salary, he couldn't afford that."

"It fit him perfectly too," Kelly called out as she wiped down the back of the sofa. "It was made for him."

Riley and I looked at each other. "Double agent?" we said simultaneously.

That wasn't too hard to imagine. As much as the CIA tried to filter out people who might turn when presented with stacks of money, one or two always slipped through the cracks.

"How well did you know him?" I asked.

Riley scowled. "Pretty well. I'd been his first handler. He did alright. Eventually they gave him to someone else. Everything I'd heard indicated he was on the up-and-up. I didn't get a good look at his clothes. Can you describe them?"

Kelly went into a detailed description that told me she took my orders to study everything to heart.

Riley's mouth dropped open, and he ran from the room, returning thirty seconds later, looking pale. "I'm kind of freaked out. Why bring the body here?"

I started to pace. "Someone knew that you were connected to him and me. They knew where you lived and how to get in without breaking in. Who could do that?"

"Oh!" Riley held up one finger and ran out of the room. He returned in an instant with a notepad. "I almost forgot. I talked to all three hotels, and it looks like a woman checked into the Sunnyside Inn the day before Rex went missing. A blonde. She gave the name Mo Knee."

"Mony?" I thought aloud. "Or Money? Either way, it's a fake name."

The Sunnyside Inn was a rather ambitious name for a tiny motel on the outskirts of town. It was a bit rundown and very cheap, and you could always count on some sort of illegal activity there, according to Rex. I'd be willing to bet there were no security cameras either.

"Did they give you a description?" I asked.

Riley shook his head. "The kid at the desk said she wore a heavy coat, hat, and huge sunglasses. Could have been a wig too. Or even a man."

"Did she have an accent?"

"No. Spoke perfect Midwestern English."

"We need to find her." Kelly joined us.

"The thing that bothers me, is that she was only here just before the wedding." I stared off into space. "That's not enough time to learn all she needed to know about Rex, me, and Riley's house." Unless it was Lana…

"She could've stayed somewhere else up until then," Kelly suggested.

"Or she's staying in another town," Riley added.

I slumped onto the couch. "At least we know this is about me. Not Rex."

Kelly joined me. "Vy Todd is a blonde. It could've been her."

I shook my head. "There's too much that's connected to me. I mean, they even killed my replacement at Langley and put the body in Riley's house. As far as I know, Harvey Oak, Prescott Winters, and Vy Todd don't even know who I am."

"Yes," Kelly mused. "But Vy Todd is related to Riley and might have found out where he lived."

Linda appeared in the doorway. "This is going to take a while, and it's getting pretty late…"

Kelly looked at her watch and jumped to her feet. "Ugh! I was supposed to be home hours ago!"

I turned to Riley. "I guess I'd better take them home. Are you going to be alright here?"

He nodded. "What about you? You shouldn't stay in your house."

I waved him off. "I'm going to find a pet sitter and move the animals to Rex's house. But I'm staying at mine so if anything happens, people know where I am."

He didn't seem to like that idea. "Which means the killers know where you are."

"Probably." I put on my coat. "Call me if you need me!"

We were on the road seconds later. I asked Kelly, "Do you know anyone who could pet sit at Rex's house for me?"

She gave me a strange look that I found suspicious. "I think I know someone. I'll call them when I get home, and then I'll send you the info."

I was too tired to ask who it was. At this point, my autopilot was on autopilot. I dropped both women off and went home.

Philby was furious. I'd been gone all day. Who was going to give her albacore tuna? She paced in front of me for ten minutes, yowling all sorts of insults that luckily I didn't understand. Martini seemed to take her side. It was hard to tell. She fell asleep halfway through my chewing out. Leonard went outside like a rocket. Poor guy. I'd kept him cooped up all day with two cats who terrorized him.

My cats hadn't been exactly welcoming to the Scottish deerhound when Rex adopted him in October. Philby liked to hide his toys, pee on his dog bed (with him still in it), and once got into his treats and while sitting out of his reach, ate each and every one in front of him. Slowly. I only found out because I checked my security cameras in the kitchen when I discovered that a brand-new bag of dog snacks was suddenly empty. Leonard got his revenge in the end. Philby was sick for two days after.

"Come on," I said as I gathered up their things. Rex already had food dishes and a cat litter box. There wasn't much else. "Let's go to Rex's."

Philby climbed over the other two as she sprinted for the door. A while back, Rex had a mouse problem, and she took every opportunity to escape to his house. She was becoming a regular escape artist, and more than once I'd found her plastered up against the outside of Rex's picture window, legs splayed as if she'd been thrown at it and stuck.

Soon, we were across the street. I collapsed on the couch, too tired to move. Maybe I'd just spend the night here. Tomorrow I could hire whoever Kelly had in mind. As I crashed, I couldn't get the image of Bobby Ray out of my head.

I mean, seriously? *That* was my replacement? A guy so stupid he was lured to Iowa from Langley for no reason? The ligature marks looked fresh enough. He wasn't killed in Virginia and brought here.

I rubbed my eyes and realized I was out of my depth here, along with Ted Weir, Kelly, and certainly Kevin. The bright spot had been the super-smart Linda Willard. But to be completely honest, I needed Rex. We all did. Of course, we needed him to solve these two murders and his own kidnapping.

Where was he?

# CHAPTER ELEVEN

———

The doorbell woke me up, and I jumped into a defensive position. I'd been fighting ninjas in my sleep, and when that happened, I usually woke up that way. I'd fallen asleep, fully clothed, on Rex's couch. I popped a mint from the candy dish into my mouth and answered the door.

A surly-looking young man stood on the steps. He was a bit on the short side and a little pudgy. I guessed he was fifteen, maybe. And he looked familiar.

The boy sighed heavily when I opened the door. "You need a pet sitter, Mrs. Wrath?"

Automatically I corrected, "It's Ms. Come in. Did Kelly Albers send you?"

The kid nodded and followed me into the house. "Nice digs."

"Thanks. This is my fiancé's house. He's a police detective."

"I know," the boy answered.

Either Kelly had told him that, or he'd been in the hot seat in Rex's office before. Not an encouraging thought.

I opened with an interview question, "Have you done this before?"

He sat on the couch, and the animals surrounded him. Leonard loved him immediately, and Martini climbed up on him and passed out—a good sign. Philby eyed him with the suspicion she usually reserved for squirrels in the yard.

The kid yawned. "Yeah. I do it all the time."

I looked at him expectantly. "For who?"

He frowned. "Most of the teachers at the high school and the principal. It's kind of a thing."

That sounded good. Apparently he didn't get in trouble in school. "What's your rate?"

"Thirty dollars a night. But I'll give you a discount since you know my sister." He rolled his eyes as if saying that hurt.

So, I knew him? "Your sister?"

The boy looked offended that I didn't know who he was. "Yeah. My sister. Betty."

I had to admit, I was torn. I loved all of my girls. And the teachers trusted him. And I really needed someone to watch the animals. On the other hand, Betty has been the evil genius behind many pranks that included dying my bangs pink as I slept and creating huge bonfires in places where bonfires shouldn't be.

"I'm so sorry," I went with. "My mind has left me for a moment. What's your name?"

"Bart."

Ah. I knew this kid. He'd faked a heart attack at a parade, which impressed Kelly, the never-impressed emergency room nurse. I needed a kid who could think on his feet like that.

"When can you start?"

He shrugged. "Immediately?"

That was when I noticed the suitcase behind him and the giant grocery bag full of junk food. How did he know I'd need him overnight? My hope was that Rex would turn up on the doorstep any minute now, happy and fine, and whisk me away to the Caribbean for a quick marriage on the beach and nothing but fruity cocktails and sun for a week.

Yes, I understand that this wasn't going to happen. Whoever had Rex wasn't going to let him go, especially with two more clues to find and solve. Over the last couple of days, my fury had been waning into frustration and fear. As a fairly impatient person, this gnawed at me, wearing me down into someone I didn't really recognize anymore.

"So." Bart cleared his throat. "What do you want me to do?"

We did a quick tour of the house, complete with the animals' feeding schedules. To his credit, the sullen teen paid attention. How much like his sister was he? It didn't matter. He was going to take care of Rex's house and the pets. That was all I needed to know. Once I got him settled in (and hid all of the weapons and matches, cuz…Betty), I went across the street and took a shower. Rex was really gone. And I had no idea where to find him.

And Betty's brother was house sitting for him.

I started to cry. It wasn't a loud, gasping-for-air cry. But tears did roll down my cheeks, and my throat ached. The reasonable side of me said this wasn't going to help anything. The flaky side of me told me to go ahead and let it out, because what else was I going to do? I sobbed through the washing of my hair until I toweled off. That was my cutoff. I had to pull it together for Rex.

In the kitchen, I threw together a quick breakfast and sat, munching on toast and eggs, as I scanned my cell for messages. Nothing from Rex. What did I expect? *Merry, it's Rex! I'm being held by Juliette in her basement. Bring an Uzi! Love you!*

Mom had sent a text two minutes ago, saying she'd driven by and there was a strange boy in Rex's backyard playing with Leonard. It was nice to know he wasn't surly all the time. I texted back telling her who it was.

Kelly asked if I'd heard from Linda yet. Officer Ted left a text asking me to call him, and Riley wondered if I'd gotten any sleep.

That was a good question, considering that I was still tired. I used to be able to sleep on anything, from army cots to the stone floor in a barn. But three years of living in an actual house with an actual bed had made me a bit soft.

*Not really*, I texted back.

I texted Kelly and asked her to get ahold of Linda. Then I called Ted Weir.

He picked up on the first ring. "Ms. Wrath! I just got a hit on the fingerprints. Can you come down to the station?"

I was there in minutes. Three minutes meant I cut through some alleys doing fifty miles an hour.

Kevin was eating SpaghettiOs out of the can with a flat-tipped screwdriver while sitting at the front desk. I didn't ask. He pointed over his shoulder. To my surprise, Ted was using Rex's office.

"I'm sorry. I should've warned you," he apologized as I stood, gaping in the doorway.

I closed my mouth. "No, no, that's fine. It's not like there are a lot of offices here." I walked in and sat down in a chair I'd always thought of as an interrogation device when Rex was in here.

"Des Moines was able to run the prints overnight. Since this involves the kidnapping of a police officer, they were in a hurry. Which helps us."

"Who was it?" I asked. "Who is the person I'm going to kill?"

He froze. "Before I tell you, you should know that you can't do anything about this. We've already picked up Vy Todd and are bringing her in."

"Vy Todd? She killed Bobby Ray Pratt?" Even though I'd thought of this, I couldn't have been more surprised if you'd told me Vladimir Putin was a classically trained ballet dancer.

Ted frowned. "I know, right? It kind of makes things more complicated."

More complicated? That was the understatement of the year. I'd been convinced for the last twenty-four hours that Lana or Leiko was behind this. Now I find out it's Vy Todd? She had no connection to me.

"It doesn't make any sense," I said. "Everything so far points to an ex-spy. Everything points to me. But this..." My mind was spinning. "It just doesn't make sense for Vy Todd to know who my replacement was at Langley. And I'm sure the CIA has nothing on Vy. So what does it mean?"

I was starting to get a bit hysterical.

Ted looked at me with sympathy in his eyes. "Tell you what. You can hide out in the observation room while I question her."

"Okay," I said. I'd been planning to do that anyway, but if this kid thought it was his idea, no skin off my nose.

He shuffled through some papers on the desk. Rex's desk. "Dr. Body sent me her reports." He frowned at the mess of papers. "They're in here somewhere. Anyway, the cause of death for Spitz was a stab wound to the heart. And Bobby Ray Pratt died from strangulation. Nothing else in there."

That was a relief, in a way. The murders were exactly as expected. No secret poisoning first or anything like that. The killer was keeping it simple. I liked simple.

"How is Linda coming along with the clue?" he asked.

"She's working on it," I said. "She'll let me know as soon as she can, and I'll tell you."

Weir rubbed his face. The poor guy looked exhausted. What a crazy indoctrination into a new job. How many policemen have to investigate their superior's kidnapping their first few months on the job? Not many, I'd bet.

"Are you okay?" I asked.

With a sigh, he sat up. "Yes. I'm fine. Sorry. This is really overwhelming. I'm so new here, I still don't understand all the procedures."

Officer Kevin Dooley walked past the doorway, carrying a live chicken. Probably his lunch.

Ted stared at the doorway. "And what's up with Dooley?" He shook his head. "The academy did not prepare me for him."

"I think he was dropped on his head as a baby. A lot. Down a long flight of stairs."

"Is it just me," he asked, "or is he always eating? We had a drug bust the other day, found some marijuana in a bag of chips at the high school. By the time the bag made it into the evidence room, the chips were gone. I had no idea what to do."

"A year ago"—I leaned forward—"Rex was raiding a teen kegger in a cornfield. They'd made pot brownies. They never made it back to the station. Kevin said it didn't affect him, but they found him sitting in the middle of the grocery store parking lot, eating a large rotisserie chicken with his hands and waving away tiny, invisible flying beagles." I hadn't been able to eat a rotisserie chicken since.

"How does he still work here?" Ted asked, his eyes wide.

I shrugged. "He got the job through his father, who was a big deal at the hospital. Somehow he made it through the academy—which is a mystery to me. Rex just says he's worked with cops who are ten times worse, and this isn't that big a deal."

The phone on his desk buzzed. He answered, agreed to something, and hung up.

"She's here." Ted pushed away from his desk and stood up. "Wait here. Once we're in the interrogation room, I'll have Officer Dooley escort you to the observation room." He looked me over. "You can't talk, shout, or do anything that would hurt the interview."

I nodded and called out "Good luck!" as he disappeared.

A minute later, Kevin walked in and grunted for me to follow him. We entered the dark room on the other side of the two-way glass, and I stared.

Vy Todd had been known as a full-figured woman who was six feet tall. But a few years in prison had not been kind to her. There wasn't one ounce of fat on her skinny bones, and her face was emaciated. Her thinning blonde hair had been tucked into a severe bun, and she did not look happy to be here.

"That's Vy Todd," Kevin said in a monotone.

"Really? I thought it was the governor." I should've been a tad less sarcastic.

Kevin looked at me with a blank face. "I don't think so. The governor is a man."

"I knew that," I said acidly. "I…" But I never finished my sentence because the interview had begun.

Ted spoke loudly, "My name is Officer Theodore Weir, and I am interviewing you, Ms. Vivienne Todd, aka Vy Todd."

Not exactly what I would've opened with, but then, I would've started with the removal of her fingernails. To each their own, I guess.

The woman sneered. "Well, get on with it then!"

Her voice was not what I'd expected. I'd expected a deep, almost masculine voice full of authority. Instead, she sounded like a child who'd inhaled too much helium. Her voice was high in pitch and sounded like her vocal chords had condensed for some reason.

"She sounds like a Munchkin from the *Wizard of Oz*." I nudged Kevin with my elbow.

He turned and looked at me. "Do you have food?"

That was when I noticed he was holding a file folder. For a moment I thought he'd eat it.

I was going to ask about the chicken from earlier, but he shrugged and turned back to the glass.

"Ms. Todd, can you give me an alibi for your whereabouts yesterday?" Ted asked, his voice cracking a little bit. I wished there was some way I could encourage him.

She laughed sharply. "I was on a beach, getting a mani pedi."

"A beach?" Ted frowned. "Where's there a beach around here?"

"You gotta be kidding me." She shrieked with laughter. "I was home all day, catching up on the shows I'd missed when I was in prison."

Ted regained his composure. "Was there anyone with you? Someone who could say you were there?"

She leaned forward with mean eyes. "*I* said I was there. That's all you need to know."

Yeah, pliers would've been much quicker. This was going to take all day. I dug into my purse and handed Kevin a bunch of dollar bills.

"Get me a chocolate candy bar and a little something for yourself."

He left before I could even put my wallet back in my purse. I'd only have a couple of minutes. Unless he wasn't very decisive. Then I'd have more. I grabbed the file Kevin had set down. Why would anyone trust this guy with any info? But bingo, I found her address. I took photos of as many pages I could until I heard the scuff of shoes outside. I was back in my spot before Kevin knew what had hit him.

"Here." He handed me a bag of chips.

Not exactly a candy bar, but at least it was edible. That was when I noticed he was eating out of a Chinese takeaway container that had *TED* written on it.

"Where's my change?" I held my hand out.

Kevin stopped eating. "I used it."

"On what?" I pointed at the carton he'd stolen from Officer Weir.

"Two bags of Corn Nuts, one Hershey Bar, and little powdered donuts," he said.

"And you're eating someone else's food?"

He looked slowly at the carton as if seeing it for the first time. "*TED* stands for Take Everything You Want."

"It says Ted. With a *D*. Not a *YW*."

"The *D* is silent."

I gave up because Ted was talking.

"How can you explain your fingerprints being at the scene of a murder yesterday?" He tried to look menacing, but it just came off as constipated.

"I don't know what you're talking about," she growled in that tiny voice.

I wasn't kidding. She sounded like she was only one foot tall.

He took a photo of Bobby Ray Pratt out of a file folder and slid it to her. "Do you recognize this man?"

She shrugged. "No. Should I?"

"He's the man who died by strangulation in a house here in Who's There. Yesterday. And your prints were on the couch where he sat."

"Look." She tossed the picture at him. "Today is the first day I've been to this stupid town. And it'll be my last."

"How do you explain having family in town?"

Oh. Right. I forgot.

The woman scoffed. "I don't have any family here."

"Riley Andrews," Ted said. "He's your second cousin, and it was his house where the body was found."

Vy leaned forward and glared at the officer. "Then maybe you'd better ask *him* why there was a dead guy on his couch."

The rest of the interview was pretty much the same. Ted threatened, and Vy blew him off. As a professional criminal, she knew not to say anything that would implicate her. As a novice detective, he was doing his best.

It didn't matter, because now I had the address where the police had picked her up. I'd pay her a visit later and show her what a real interrogation looked like.

"I'm gonna head out." I yawned. "Enjoy Ted's lunch," I added.

Kevin nodded. "Okay."

My cell went off as soon as I got into my car. Rex! The caller ID said it was coming from *Sexi Rexi*, a nickname he didn't know I'd given him.

"Rex! Where are you? Are you alright? How can I find you?" The words spilled from my lips like Niagara Falls. Then I realized he hadn't said anything.

"Rex?" I cried.

He hung up. Or his captor did. Why risk calling? If I'd had my wits about me, I could've traced the call. Was the killer/kidnapper becoming impatient that I wasn't solving the clues fast enough? And if so, did that mean they might kill Rex off sooner than planned? I couldn't let that happen!

There was a long list of suspects, including some that didn't even make sense. It was time to take one of them off the list.

Juliette Dowd's house was a small ranch with white walls and green shutters. The woman always wore green suits. She took her job at the Girl Scout Council very seriously. Was she home? It was eleven in the morning on a weekday. There was no car in the driveway. In fact, tire tracks in the fresh snow indicated she'd left. There wasn't another set that said she'd come back.

I got out of the car and walked down the sidewalk, turning at the corner and again into the alley behind the house. The detached garage was empty. She really wasn't there. But for how long?

I wasn't really in the right frame of mind for a break-in. It's probably more honest to say this was a bad idea. Fortunately, I didn't care. I pulled on my gloves and walked confidently up to the house. My short dirty blonde hair was stuffed under my stocking cap. It would be difficult to ID me if there was a nosy neighbor watching. And in a small town like this, there was always a nosy neighbor watching. Sometimes, that was me.

The back door was unlocked. I hesitated. Who didn't lock their door when they left? Was she home? Maybe her car was in the shop, and she was dropped off here to wait it out. I did the only thing I could do. I knocked.

Then I ducked behind a huge rain barrel and waited.

The seconds ticked by, and no one came to the door. Just to be safe, I repeated the process and waited. When no one came to the door, I realized Juliette was just stupid and had left her door unlocked.

It was an invitation that was hard to turn down. I stepped inside and found myself in a bright and cheery kitchen. The wallpaper consisted of sunny yellow flowers, and the appliances were bright red. The fridge was plastered with pictures of teddy bears and ponies.

It was a lot different than I'd expected. I figured her more for the satanic rituals–type—broken dolls with gouged out eyes all over the floor. I guess you never know. Like Vy Todd's munchkin voice. People can surprise you.

Over the course of my short career, I'd met everything from a one-legged soccer star to a zoologist who was allergic to every animal on the planet. And once, in La Paz, I had to work with a magician who was terrified of magic. His best trick? Sawing a stuffed rabbit in half. And believe it or not, his act had thousands of followers. He's retired now and living like a king in Toledo.

Leaving the spotless kitchen behind, I ventured into Juliette's dining room and found total chaos. The chairs and table were upended and smashed. A china hutch lay on its side, vomiting broken porcelain. The living room was the same, only this time, someone had taken a knife to the upholstery for a little tummy tuck.

Something was wrong. Unless she lived like this, which seemed unlikely after the sunshine and rainbows kitchen, I'd say something bad had happened here. I picked up my pace and jogged through the rest of the house, calling out for Juliette.

Sure, I'd broken in, but if she was tied up and gagged somewhere, maybe she'd cut me a little slack for rescuing her. The bedroom, guest room, and bathroom were gutted and destroyed. Every room I entered had been destroyed, but I found no screaming, hateful redhead.

I ran for the stairs and took them two at a time on the way down to the basement. There was no point in sneaking around anymore. The lower level had been unfinished, but in the middle of the room was a chair with rope lying around it.

A red spot drew my attention, and I dropped to my knees. Blood. Something bad had happened. I'd originally thought I'd find Rex here, but instead I found something else.

The question was, had she had Rex here originally? The strands of long red hair stuck in the rope made me think otherwise. Someone had held Juliette captive in her own house. And then they'd moved her.

Juliette Dowd was missing. And to my complete surprise, I wasn't responsible for it.

# CHAPTER TWELVE

————

My cell buzzed. I looked around to make sure I was alone, which made me feel a little silly because, of course I was. I certainly wasn't inhibited by Juliette Dowd's presence.

I didn't recognize the number but answered anyway.

"Hey, Mrs. Wrath." Bart's monotone slacker voice floated into my ear.

"Bart?" I frowned at the cell. "Is something wrong? Are the animals alright?"

"Yeah. I just wanted to know if I can eat some of your chips." I heard explosions in the background, which had to be a movie.

There was no time to quiz him. "Eat whatever you want. Have to go. Bye." I hung up.

Poor kid. I hadn't told him he could eat. At least he'd asked. That was refreshing. My girls usually attacked any food laid out like a swarm of pyromaniac locusts.

My cell buzzed again.

"Can I have something to drink?" Bart asked. "We didn't specify beverages when you said I could eat what I wanted."

My patience was starting to wear thin. "As long as it's not alcohol, knock yourself out. Now I really have to go."

"Whatever," he said before hanging up.

I poked around the basement to look for clues, and because I could. Who knew what that woman had here? Everything was neatly displayed in boxes on shelves. What did I expect? The skulls of her enemies? Weapons of mass destruction? Volleyballs?

Sadly, all I could find were boxes of Girl Scout brochures. Either she worked from home, or she was stealing marketing supplies from the council. It didn't matter, because at least she didn't have a box labeled *Ways to Destroy Merry Wrath.*

Now what? I'd promised Ted I'd let the police know when I stumbled onto something. I didn't want to interrupt him if he was still with Vy Todd, so I texted to tell him what I'd found at Juliette's house, without explaining why I was here.

My cell buzzed. *Grrrr...*

"Bart! I don't care if you eat the silverware!" I shouted.

"Merry?" Linda asked.

"Oh! I'm so sorry, Linda. My pet sitter has been calling me every five minutes…"

She interrupted, "Never mind that. Can you come to my condo?"

I assured her that I could and fled the scene just as I heard sirens in the distance. I left the door unlocked so they could get in without any trouble, because I was helpful like that.

My old teacher answered on the first knock. "I have the whole clue unscrambled. I'm working on the crossword now, but it's harder than the last one and will take a little longer."

"What's the clue?"

"We knew it would have the words *something borrowed* in it," Linda said as she led me to the kitchen table, "which made it easier. Here's what it says,"

*There will be no honeymoon tomorrow…Let's turn next to Something Borrowed.*

A jolt of pain shot through me. Was the killer saying that Rex could die tomorrow?

"We're running out of time," I croaked.

Linda nodded. "Well then, I'd better get back to work."

This crossword puzzle looked like the other. Linda had done an amazing job and was more than halfway done.

"Can I help? Like last time?"

She took in my begging eyes and offered, "I don't know. You're welcome to look at the clues I haven't crossed out yet."

Leaning over her shoulder, I tried to make sense of the one- and two-word clues. This really wasn't my thing. Who knew I'd need to know how to solve crosswords to save my fiancé's life?

Like the other puzzle, this one probably had numbers written out as words—which would make the clue extra long. I watched for a while but started to get agitated. It drove me nuts that I was so helpless.

Why couldn't the killer have just taken out a billboard announcing where Rex was? That would be convenient and very nice of him. Instead, we were worrying ourselves sick over these puzzles. Well, I was.

"The clues are getting harder," Linda explained after my fifth or forty-seventh pity sigh. She pointed to number three across. "The answer has five letters, all of which are highlighted, and I've tried a number of options."

Something popped into my head. "Class?"

Linda wrote it down. "I think my brain is beginning to give out on me. I should've caught that."

"Does that mean the word *class* is part of the clue?" I asked eagerly.

"I don't know. Remember, all the letters in the highlighted boxes have to be unscrambled. We won't know until the end. Chances are"—she gave me a small smile—"it isn't."

I pulled up a chair and sat down. "You know, I haven't thanked you for all of this."

Linda put her hand over mine. It felt like a hug. "I'm happy to help. This is something I can do. Besides, I haven't had this much adventure in years."

"Do you miss teaching?"

She looked off into space for a moment. "I do, and I don't. I miss the kids like you. The ones who made a difference. I miss the kids I was able to help—the kids who needed it the most. But that was a long time ago. I'm happy where I am right now."

I put my hand over hers. "Well, you made a difference in my life then, and now."

Linda laughed. "Wait to thank me when we have your handsome detective back."

My cell buzzed for what felt like the hundredth time today. It was Riley.

"Merry?" he asked. "Can you come down to my office? I might have something."

"Are you good to go here? I can stay if you need me."

My teacher shook her head. "Go. I'll call when I have this solved."

I said good-bye to Linda and headed out.

*  *  *

"Did you find something?" I asked as I pushed the door open.

Riley looked up from a bunch of papers and frowned. "I don't know. It's kind of confusing."

I sat next to him and immediately recognized the pages as satellite surveillance images.

"You called in a favor?"

He nodded. "I have a contact who sent these. They're Lana's movements since she was released. I guess they put a tracker in her last meal. I'm surprised it hasn't passed out of her system yet."

"Yeah," I said a little snappishly. "That's interesting and all, but I don't care about her digestion. Is she in the US or what?"

"I guess the answer to that is *or what*," he said.

He pointed to a map that spanned her movements over the last forty-eight hours.

"She's been to Paris, Beijing, and Hawaii in two days?" I scowled. "That's not right."

Riley sighed. "It's the latest technology. It's one hundred percent accurate."

"But that makes no sense," I insisted. "It takes hours to fly from one of those places to the other. I doubt it's possible."

"Technically." Riley rubbed his eyes. "In answer to your question, she is in the US since she's in Hawaii."

"She could be anywhere," I complained. "I don't think this is her. They must've found the tracker and are screwing with the satellite download."

He nodded. "And Leiko hasn't turned up. But there have been sightings in three countries already."

"So she could be anywhere too." I ran my hands through my hair."

My cell went off. I thought about throwing it across the room. It was Bart's number.

"Yes?" I sighed as I answered.

"Yeah, Mrs. Wrath?" Bart's monotone never strayed. "There are two really old people here. They said they're checking on the animals. Said they're your parents, but I'm not sure. Should I ask for ID?"

"Hand the phone to the woman." I waited a second until I heard my mother's voice. "Sorry, Mom. I hired Betty's brother to keep an eye on the animals while I'm running around town."

"It's okay, kiddo!" she said cheerily. "I just wanted to let you know we have to go back to DC. The Senate is calling for an important vote, and your dad wants to be there."

"Do you need me to give you a ride to the airport?" I felt guilty hoping the answer would be no.

"Absolutely not. I'm sorry to be leaving you at this time. I can stay if you'd like." Worry hung heavy in her voice.

"Go home with Dad. I've got this," I lied.

She wasn't buying it. "Are you sure, kiddo? Because I can stay…"

"Mom," I insisted. "Go home. There's nothing you can do. I'm grateful you've been here all this time, but I've got all kinds of people helping me. I promise you'll be the first to know when we find Rex."

We said our good-byes, and Mom promised to call once they were home.

I turned to Riley. "Where does this leave us?"

"We have to do some surveillance."

I filled him in on Juliette's disappearance. "Do you think this is all connected?"

"How could it not be?" Riley mused. "Rex and Juliette are connected to each other and to you. I just don't understand why they kidnapped her. She said she was searching Rex's house for evidence that you took him, right?"

I nodded. "Do you think she found something that made the killer take notice?"

"What could she find at Rex's house?" He stared into space.

I shrugged. "I don't even know if that's where they took him from or if it was somewhere else." With a shock, I remembered, "He called me! Well, his cell did. There was no voice on the other end."

Riley frowned. "Either the killer is taunting you…"

I finished his sentence. "…or Rex was able to get free to call."

"I can ping his phone." Riley jumped up and ran to his computer. "Cell phone towers! They record where and when a call is made. We know the when and to whom. Hand me your phone!"

I handed it over and looked over his shoulder at the monitor. "Isn't this information hard to get? Don't you need a court order?"

He shook his head, "I've hacked into their system. Now, what provider does Rex use, and what's the cell number?"

After I gave him the info, Riley plugged it in, and suddenly the screen was filled with phone numbers. We located Rex's. He'd only used the phone once since he'd been taken. Would this lead us to Rex?

My stomach flip-flopped, and my palms began to sweat. We could find him today! By the end of today, I could have Rex in my arms, surrounded by the dead person or persons who took him!

"Where did it ping?" I asked as I vibrated in place.

Riley wrote down an address and grabbed his coat. He locked the door, and we climbed into my van, racing toward the corner of Brown Street and Twelfth Avenue.

"By the way," I said as I drove way too quickly, "they found Vy's fingerprints in your house where the body was found."

Riley looked startled. "She was in my house? No. That's impossible. I reviewed the surveillance tape."

I slammed on the brakes and turned to him. "You have hidden video and didn't tell me?"

He held up his hands defensively. "There's nothing on it. One second there's nothing, and then there's a blip and Bobby Ray's body just sort of appears."

I hit the gas and launched the van almost into the air. "Crap."

"Someone tampered with the digital recording when they were at my house."

That was possible. There was no such thing as the perfect device in Spy Land. For every major breakthrough, whether it was the world's most powerful listening device or something that made rats explode, there was someone who could render it powerless.

"It has to be Lana," I grumped. "Leiko, Vy Todd, and the other crooks couldn't possibly know how to do that."

I really, really didn't want it to be Lana. She hated me. Like, really hated me. And I didn't want to go up against a spy who was still in the biz. Not after years as a civilian.

"Not necessarily. Vy could have someone who works for her who can do that."

"We have to find Lana. Prove that she's here or in Russia." I couldn't stand this much longer.

"I've got a couple of guys working on it at Langley," he said.

"Who? I know everyone who worked in Russia. That was one of our areas, remember?"

He arched an eyebrow. "You didn't know Bobby Ray. And he took your old beat."

"Who's working on it?" I asked again. We were getting close to the intersection.

Riley looked for a moment like he wasn't going to answer me. "Edgar and Al."

This time I slammed on the brakes and put the van in park. "Edgar and Al are idiots! They don't speak Russian! They speak Slovenian!"

"They went through intensive language training. They're fine." He sounded a bit defensive.

He had a right to be. Edgar and Al were two guys who joined the CIA together, went through training together, and somehow ended up together. It was unusual for a couple of new agents to get the same assignment, and it came out later that these two had been friends since middle school band camp.

At any rate, they'd almost been killed dozens of times. How it didn't go all the way to dead, I didn't know. These two walked into traps like they were lobotomized lemmings. They'd gone through four sets of handlers in one year, which was extremely unusual. These guys had been pretty controversial at Langley because they were such a liability. And now Riley was getting intel from them?

"Find someone else," I snapped. "Someone good."

"I can't do that. I've been out of the biz too, remember? I've a limited number of resources to pull from."

We rode in silence. He was right, but I wasn't happy about it. Of course I wanted the best of the best working on Rex's case. However, anyone who did that for us at the CIA could lose their jobs or worse. And by worse, I meant getting stationed in the Arctic Circle. Unless you're into eating seal blubber and being cold all the time, that was the one assignment everyone dreaded.

I'd parked half a block from the intersection, so we jumped out of the van and ran to the corner. Dusk was hitting. The sun was gone by five in the afternoon in the winter.

"There's nothing here," Riley said as he turned completely around.

He was right. We were at the edge of town, by four empty lots. At one time there'd been a butcher shop, a barbershop, a gas station, and a long time ago, a rumored brothel. The brothel mysteriously burned down in the 1940s. The other places were around through the '90s but torn down in 2000.

"Maybe they were transporting him?" Riley pulled the printout from his coat pocket and tried to study it in the darkness.

I was circling the intersection, looking for anything that might have been left behind. Could Rex have thrown something from the car if what Riley had said was true? It didn't seem likely, considering a window down in winter would be a tad suspicious.

Turning my attention to the lot on my right, I started a perimeter search. We'd had a snowfall recently, and the snow was pristine. Untouched. If someone had walked through here, we'd know it.

"Nothing!" I screamed. "There's *nothing here*!"

I started kicking the snow and cursing. Loudly. A few cars slowed down to watch this psycho woman throwing a temper tantrum in the midst of a vacant lot, but I was on a roll now. I started making snowballs and threw them at the street sign.

"*Arrrrrrgh!*" I shrieked when I (of course) missed.

I can throw a knife with deadly accuracy, but a snowball was beyond my talent range. Finally I resorted to thrashing and screaming in place until Riley ran over and hugged me close against him.

And that was when I started crying. Loud, panicked sobs with huge intakes of air in between. My whole body shook uncontrollably, and the whole while, Riley gently rocked me back and forth, patting my back and speaking soothingly. I didn't even know what he was saying, but it seemed to help, because after a few minutes, I was able to breath normally again.

"It's alright," Riley said softly. "It will be alright."

I pushed away, and he handed me a tissue. After wiping my face, I stuffed it into my pocket.

"Will it be alright? Because things don't seem to be going that way," I hiccupped.

Riley looked at me with serious eyes. "Honestly? I can't say. But I'm going to do everything I can to see that you and Rex get a happy ending."

I almost lost it again. Standing there, my feet frozen by the snow, my breath billowing in midair, I wondered.

And that was when I got hit in the face with a snowball.

Riley stood there with a grin. "What? The cold will keep your face from getting puffy."

I grabbed a handful of snow and stuffed it down his shirt. He screamed. I laughed.

"You okay now?" he said as he danced around, trying to get the snow out of his shirt.

"No." I shook my head. "But I'm pulling myself together so we can move on."

Back in the van, Riley made me crank the heat. I took several deep breaths and steeled myself. I was going to find Rex. Alive. And maybe, just maybe, Juliette. I couldn't guarantee that she'd survive.

My cell buzzed. Bart.

"Hey, Bart," I said with fake cheer. "What's up?"

"So," he droned, "did you want me to spend the night, or what?"

I was beyond mentally and physically exhausted.

"Is that okay?" I asked.

"Yeah," he said without one single speck of emotion. "Mom said she'd bring me my Xbox."

"That would be great, Bart. Thank you. I don't know how long this will take."

"'Sokay. I'm charging for a whole day, so…" And with that, he hung up.

\* \* \*

I made it home, ate a whole bag of Pizza Rolls, and took a long, hot shower. I barely hit the pillow before I fell asleep. My last thoughts were that I was going to rescue Rex and kill whoever was behind this. I fell asleep with sweet dreams of revenge.

\* \* \*

"Mrs. Wrath!" Betty's voice must've been part of a dream I'd been having where I was following a scent-trained armadillo into a dark warehouse.

A sharp poke in the shoulder made me realize this wasn't a dream.

"She's not dead!" Betty shouted, and my eyes flew open.

Ten little girls ran into the bedroom, followed by Kelly.

"Quit letting the girls into my house in the morning!" I grumbled.

"Where are the cats?" Hannah asked.

"And Leonard?" Inez pressed.

Betty puffed up. "My brother is babysitting them at Detective Ferguson's house."

The girls stared at her.

"Have you been there?" asked one of the Kaitlyns.

"Did you find his gun?" Lauren added.

I started to sit up and realized I'd been so tired I had gone to bed naked.

"Kelly," I said in a calm voice. "Why don't you take the girls into the kitchen?"

The girls looked at me questioningly.

"I've got ice cream sandwiches..." I didn't even need to finish my sentence over the stampede that emptied out my room.

Kelly closed the door behind her, and I quickly got dressed. I wasn't really sure how many ice cream sandwiches I actually had, so my time might be limited. It turned out I had a case of the things. By the time I joined them, Kelly was protesting the girls having their third sandwich. I snagged one and peeled off the wrapper.

"I can't believe you are giving them ice cream in the winter, at nine a.m.!" Kelly hissed.

"That's what you get for bringing them into my bedroom before I'm up."

Kelly led me into the living room, but not before I grabbed another ice cream sandwich.

"This was the girls' idea. They were worried about you. And they wanted to do something to cheer you up."

I softened. "Awww. They're great kids. I just can't justify any time away from this investigation. If I could, I'd search for Rex 24/7."

She nodded. "I know. It was just so sweet for them to offer. That, and it's the last day of the holiday break, and their parents wanted them out of the house."

"I guess we could send them on a scavenger hunt, door-to-door to find Rex," I mused. "I've still got a couple sparkly Rex unicorn posters somewhere..."

Kelly ignored my suggestion. "Any news?"

I told Kelly about Lana and Leiko. Considering that due to me, she'd had run-ins with them in the past, she wasn't too happy. By the time I caught her up on all the latest, she looked like she was regretting bringing the girls here.

"If this is about you, we have to get the girls out of here. They may not be safe."

I shook my head. "The killer/kidnapper wants me to solve the clues first. Nothing is going to happen until the Blue clue."

Kelly didn't look convinced. "Let's assume they're the ones who took Juliette Dowd. Why wouldn't they do something to the girls? They went after Rex, so why not other people close to you?"

"Well, if they took Juliette because they thought she was close to me, then the joke is on them." I wandered back into the kitchen, but sadly all the ice cream novelties were gone.

The girls were starting to short out from sugar overload. We needed to do something fast before they started climbing the walls. But whatever we did would be taking away from the investigation. I needed to keep pushing on. But how? And that was when I had the best idea ever.

*  *  *

"Why are we here?" Kelly looked around the playground in the heart of Des Moines.

The girls were running around, hitting each other with snowballs, and rolling deformed snowmen. They had a collective look in their eyes not too different from a man I once spotted in Kabul dressed as the Easter Bunny after taking a whole lot of PCP.

"It's probably better if you didn't know," I said.

She stepped in front of me. "You haven't taken your eyes off of that house since we arrived."

"Don't point at it!" I snatched her arm back.

She folded her arms over her chest. "Who are you surveilling?"

I waved her off. "It's no one. Not really. Just a suspect."

"Just a suspect in a double kidnapping who has murdered two people?"

"When you say it like that, it does sound bad. I like my definition better." I kicked at some snow with the toe of my boot.

My best friend glared at me. "Either you tell me who it is, or I'm going over there and knocking on that door."

To be honest, I was a little torn. Kelly could take on anyone. Soo Jin once saw her throw a three-hundred-pound junkie to the floor and subdue him in the emergency room. But as much as I liked those odds, I decided to come clean.

"Vy Todd lives there."

Kelly turned an interesting shade of red. "You brought the troop to a park across the street from a drug smuggler who's suspected of killing several people!"

"Relax. It's totally safe. This is a really nice neighborhood, and we're in a park with kids."

"You're using the girls as cover?" Kelly shrieked this time.

Betty and Lauren heard that and came running.

"What are we cover for?" Lauren twisted into some interesting fighting formations. "Is it the bad guys who took Detective Ferguson? Are we going to fight?" The girl reared back and kicked her foot all the way through a snowman. Kelly had to help her extricate herself.

"Don't be ridiculous." Betty rolled her eyes. "You can't go into hand-to-hand combat with someone like that. You need this." She pulled a zip gun from her pocket.

I threw myself onto the girl, half burying her in the snow. By the time we got to our feet, I had the zip gun. Which was good, because if things went bad with my partially formed plan, we might have a shootout.

Huh. Now that I thought about it, maybe this wasn't such a good idea.

That was when things got interesting.

Prescott Winters III came strolling down the sidewalk. The wealthy wife killer (and possible parent killer) completely ignored us as he passed. Kelly and the girls had no idea who he was, but I'd been doing a little online research. I could spot that tall, thin frame with its weasel face anywhere.

Under the pretense of helping Betty up, which I was sure I would've done anyway, I watched him. He had no interest in us whatsoever. Which was good because to my complete surprise, he walked up to Vy Todd's house and rang the doorbell. Seconds later, the woman appeared at the door, and after looking both ways, let him in.

"Did you see that?" I hissed. "That was Prescott Winters III!"

Kelly's head swiveled. "That guy who just walked by?"

I nodded. "He just went into Vy's house! She let him in! Stop looking!"

She turned back to me. "We should probably call Officer Weir and let him know."

"He's at least half an hour away!" I protested. "I need to get closer."

Betty finished brushing herself off. "I'm on it!"

Without waiting for me to ask what she was *on*, the little girl tore off down the sidewalk toward the house where the dangerous criminals were.

"No!" I shouted as I chased after her. "Wait!"

Kelly stayed with the other girls, but when they noticed Betty on the run, they joined in. I'm not proud to say that a couple of them passed me. I regretted eating all that ice cream for breakfast.

Betty stopped just short of the house. She bent down and dug through the snow until she found a rock. She started packing snow around it, and before I could reach her, hurled it at a window in Vy Todd's house.

The other girls sensed something was up, so they started throwing snowballs at each other. I had to admit, it was an excellent cover.

Vy came running out of the house, screaming at the girls. Prescott came out as far as the porch, and someone joined him. It was Harvey Oak! I'd all but ruled him out! But here they were, Rex's Most Wanted, together! I pulled my hat lower on my face and pulled my scarf up in an attempt to disguise myself a little. Just in case I needed to confront them later. I didn't want them tying me to the girls.

"Whatever you do," I whispered, "don't laugh."

The childlike munchkin voice shrieked, "What are you brats doing?" Vy Todd stormed over, reminding me that I had more pressing matters to deal with.

A couple of the girls bit quivering lips, but for the most part, they acted like her voice was totally normal. For a brief second, I thought my warning might've triggered suspicion as Vy stared for just a second, waiting for giggles. When they didn't come, she regained her outrage.

"I'm so sorry!" I slipped between her and the girls. "Things got out of hand! I'll pay for your window."

She shook her fists. "I should have you locked up! Juvenile delinquents!"

Betty stepped forward with big, watery eyes. "I'm so sorry, ma'am! Please don't call the police!"

I didn't know what surprised me more, Vy Todd's little cabal or Betty pretending to be sad and vulnerable. The kid's skills were getting spooky.

I had an idea. "Let me come in and see the damage. I can have my insurance agent here in twenty minutes to look at it." I waited to see if she'd take me up on it.

The woman hesitated. She looked back toward the doorway, and Harvey and Prescott dove back into the house.

"Um, no. That's okay. It was just an accident." She started to back up with her hands out in front of her. "Just try to be more careful!" The woman turned and ran back inside her house, slamming the door.

"Well?" Betty looked up at me with dry eyes.

"Well what?" I asked.

"Now that the window's broken, we can hide in the hedges and listen to what's going on. Let's go."

I couldn't have been more proud if she was my own kid. The only problem was I figured ten girls and two adults wouldn't fit under that window.

Kelly joined us, hyperventilating. "That's enough for today!"

That was all well and good, but how was she going to convince them to walk away? She gave me a wink.

"Who wants lunch? I happen to know a great place one block over with hot dogs and french fries!"

The screams brought people out onto their porches. Once they noticed our group, they went back inside.

"You go do what you have to do," Kelly whispered. "I'll take the girls."

"Thank you!" I hugged her.

She arched one eyebrow. "Oh, don't thank me yet." She held out her hand. "This is on you."

I probably deserved that. I handed over my credit card and slipped behind a tree as they all marched away. Loud voices came from the broken window. This was my chance. Keeping to the shoveled sidewalk, I walked across the street and passed the house, doubling back through the side yard into some large hedges under the window.

My only problem was the footprints in the snow that gave me away. Maybe I could smudge them on my way out.

"I'm not sure this is a good idea," one of the men said.

I didn't know the difference between Prescott's and Harvey's voices. Quietly, I slid my cell phone from my pocket and set it to record. Then I held it up as close to the window as I could and prayed it would capture the conversation.

"Oh," said an affected voice with a snooty, cultured accent. Definitely Prescott. "I don't know. I rather like it."

Did that mean they were just getting together now? Did that mean they didn't have Rex? I had too little information to go on to decide.

"Sit down, Vy!" Harvey snarled. "Your pacing is making me nervous!"

The woman shrieked, "Those…girls…I could kill those girls!"

Hey! That was a bit over the top.

"Who cares about that?" Prescott said. "Do sit down. Forget about those urchins."

"Fine!" she snapped, and I heard what sounded like a thud. She wasn't a large woman but could apparently drop onto furniture like a sullen, preteen elephant.

"You haven't mentioned my favorite word yet," Prescott said. "Money."

"Yeah," Harvey said. "We get that this is about revenge and all that. But revenge doesn't pay the bills."

The three of them were going to get revenge? It seemed like I had them, but the timeline was all wrong. Rex had already been kidnapped and three clues discovered. Had Vy taken matters into her own hands and was now trying to bring Oak and Winters on board?

"Don't worry about that. It's lucrative enough for you," she spat.

"Where do we do this?" Harvey asked.

Uh-oh. Do what? Kill Rex? And how would that make them any money?

"We can't move the item now," Vy's munchkin voice said. "I'm getting some heat from the cops in that sad little town."

A wave of relief washed over me. Okay, if the item was Rex, that meant she was keeping him alive until she could do whatever. I had a little time yet.

And that was when my cell went off. It didn't buzz. It rang. The *Dora the Explorer* theme song was my ringtone, and I hit the screen, dropped the zip gun, and ran like hell toward the back of the house. I kept running up an alley until I felt that I'd gotten away. Then I circled the park through the alleys of the houses fronting it, hoping the zip gun would draw suspicion away from me and the girls, because who suspects little girls of having zip-guns? Well, Betty not included.

I found the troop inside a 1950s-themed diner, eating what looked like a couple dozen hot dogs, while a waiter on roller skates flirted and teased. I slid into the booth and ordered a footlong with chili and cheese, cheese fries, and a chocolate shake. The waiter grinned and skated away.

The good news was that if the three criminals tracked us down, we had a pretty ironclad alibi since the girls came here straight away. The waiter would probably include me in the entourage that had been here the whole time, especially if I tipped him well.

But no one came looking for us. And the footlong was so good I had another one, and we all finished with banana splits.

I had digital evidence. Betty made me proud, and ate a whole lot of junk food. Rex wouldn't like any of this, but all in all, things were looking up.

# CHAPTER THIRTEEN

———

"Best winter vacation ever!" Ava shouted for the fifth time as she punched the ceiling of my van.

I had to agree. It was dark now, but we were heading back to Who's There with some valuable information. For once I felt like we had a break in the case.

"Did you get some good intel?" Betty leaned forward conspiratorially.

I had her, Ava, and the four Kaitlyns in my van. I'd wanted to thank her for her quick thinking without Kelly around to disapprove.

"Yes, I did." I beamed. "You did a great job out there!"

Betty sat back—didn't smile but nodded. "I'll settle for a reference letter to join the CIA. After college though. I'll need a good cover, so I'm majoring in international business."

"Really?" was all I could think to say.

"Yeah. I'm taking an online class in Arabic. Mom and Dad don't know about that. I used Bart's debit card to pay for it."

I know that I should probably discourage her from this behavior but opted instead for paying Bart a bonus.

"He hasn't noticed?" I asked.

"No. He never checks his account balance online. It wouldn't matter if he did. I've hacked it anyway." The girl found a pen in my glove box and began endlessly clicking it. Was she wondering how many ways she could kill a man with a pen? By the way, it's fourteen.

"You're hacking banks now?" Okay, now I should say something.

She looked thoughtful, stepping up the speed with which she was clicking the pen. "Not the bank. Just his emailed monthly statements. That he doesn't read. But you can never be too sure, right?"

"Um." My mind raced, searching for the right thing to say. "What are you going to do if he finds you out?"

Betty stopped clicking the pen. "I haven't really thought that far. I'll work on it."

It wasn't that Betty was a major troublemaker in the troop—she wasn't. Well, not *the* major troublemaker at least. The girl was smart, quirky, and terrifyingly confident and liked to motivate the troop with war speeches from *Patton* and *300*. Sure, she did some things from time to time that made Kelly's head spin. But I had a soft spot in my heart for her. She'd make an amazing field agent. Too bad the CIA didn't have a junior division.

"Can I have my zip gun back?" She looked me in the eyes.

"About that," I said slowly. "Where did you get a zip gun? Did you know they're illegal?"

"I made it," she said simply. "It wasn't hard."

I gave her a look. "Yeah, you're not getting it back. And please don't bring another one to anything ever."

Betty shrugged. "Okay."

There should be a Scout badge for improvised weapons. Zip guns weren't easy to make, which meant Betty's brain was scary. Hers actually looked like a gun, with a rudimentary wood frame and some metal pieces. I've used flashlights, pipes, and one time I was able to fashion a zip gun using a coat hanger, a lipstick tube, and aluminum foil.

The girls launched into a medley of Scout songs, and I wondered what Officer Weir was going to think of my little investigation at Vy Todd's house. I probably bent a law or two, and I didn't want to get into trouble. I could send it anonymously. Or I could just be up front about it.

Like he was about the investigation at Juliette's house? Why hadn't I heard anything? We'd agreed to share information. Yes, I know. I didn't exactly let him know before I broke into the redheaded psycho's house. And I kind of ran off to Des Moines half-cocked.

Communication was a two-way street, and in some cases, a three-way street, but only in Brazil. The best thing to do would be to sit down with him and go over what I had. He was a rookie and young. It was up to me to be the adult. Rex would want that.

"Mrs. Wrath!" Ava called out from the back seat. "Mrs. Albers wants to talk to you!"

She handed her phone to Betty, who thoughtfully hit the speaker button. I immediately warned Kelly that she was on speaker, so saying anything could cause trouble.

She seemed breathless. "Linda called. She's solved the puzzle!"

It felt like everything had stopped suddenly, including my breathing. We were so close! Rex was so close! There was no way I was going to wait one more minute. We were going to solve this. I just knew it.

"Girls," I said, "we're making a quick stop."

Kelly hung up. I handed back Ava's cell phone, and the girls started texting their parents to explain the detour. The girls' folks were used to this kind of thing. They didn't really care how long I kept their kids, which seemed like a good and bad thing. At any rate, it wouldn't be a problem.

"Who's Linda?" Betty asked.

"She was my fourth-grade teacher," I said. "She's very good at puzzles and is helping me find Detective Ferguson."

"Oh. So she's kind of like you are to us?"

I thought about that for a moment and tried to picture Linda Willard making ghillie suits for sniper practice or allowing the girls to go through two boxes of matches because they loved starting fires.

"Kind of," I replied. "Except she's more responsible."

"Did you like her?" Ava asked. "I like my teacher. She doesn't yell at us…much."

"Yes," I answered. "She was one of my favorite teachers."

"Why?" asked one of the Kaitlyns.

"Well, she gave us amazing books to read and taught us to work hard. She knew we could handle whatever she had us do, which gave us confidence."

"Sounds like a lot of work," Betty grumbled.

"It was, but it was worth it. I was proud of everything I did in that class because I worked at it. It didn't come easily. Nothing should come easily."

"What about cotton candy?" piped up another Kaitlyn. "Cotton candy should come easily."

"Um, I'm not sure that fits what I'm saying…"

"I wish I had some cotton candy now," said one of the other Kaitlyns, and the others agreed.

"Was your teacher nice?" Betty asked.

I nodded. "She was very nice. Tough but nice. If you did your part, you were rewarded with one of her smiles. We all worked hard to get that smile."

"That's it? No trophy or anything?" Betty seemed scandalized. "We get trophies for everything these days."

And that was the problem with this generation. "What's the point of getting a prize just for doing what everyone else is doing?"

Betty rolled her eyes. "Cuz it's a prize! Duh!"

"A prize that you worked for that is the only one of its kind is way better than everyone getting a prize just for being there." I felt proud dispensing a little wisdom.

She looked at me for a moment. "You've lost me."

My mind raced for an analogy and found one. "Well, think about the Halloween parade. We've won first prize three years in a row, right?"

Betty nodded. "The first prize trophy is way bigger than the others."

"That's what made it so special," I said. "It would've been okay to win second place, but we worked hard and, in the face of several adversities, pulled together and won."

She frowned. "It was hard work. We had to come up with something fast when our float was wrecked."

"That's right. We could've given up or done something lame. But we didn't. We worked on it until the last minute. Didn't that make the win better?"

The girl was silent for a moment, the wheels turning in her head. That was when I noticed that Ava and the Kaitlyns had been listening. Good. Maybe like Linda taught me, I could teach these girls a valuable lesson.

"Okay. That makes sense. I guess you're right," Betty said at last, and the other girls responded by cheering. "Bigger is better, after all."

As they launched back into some Girl Scout songs, I felt a little swell of pride. Was this how Linda felt when the class did well? It was a wonderful feeling. I could get addicted to this.

We pulled up into Linda's driveway, and I left the car running and ran inside. Out of the corner of my eye, I saw Kelly get out of her van and walk over to talk to the girls in mine.

The door opened before I got there.

"I solved it." She handed me the piece of paper. "I don't know what it means, but it looks like we have to move quickly."

I read the clue.

*Down the street is where you meet. Hurry before you miss your treat.*

"I know what it means!" I ran to the van and got in.

Linda climbed into Kelly's van, and we took off. I loved that she wanted to be part of this. Linda totally had my back. The girls in my van seemed to know something was up, because they were very quiet. How could I explain this to them?

My brain was in save-Rex mode, however, and I probably wasn't thinking very clearly. For now, the troop was with us, and there wasn't much to do about it. Wait! What if there was a dead body? Corpses had popped up for the other clues. Why wouldn't there be one here?

A few minutes later, we were pulling up in front of the elementary school where my troop met. I told the girls and Kelly to wait with the vehicles. If someone had been murdered, I didn't want them involved. Linda jumped out of the van and followed me inside. I didn't try to stop her.

From a distance, I could see that a light was on in the room where my troop had meetings. To my surprise, the front door to the school was open. My senses were on alert for a trap, but I didn't stop until I burst into the classroom.

No one living or dead was there. The lights were all on. Where was my *treat*? I began to search the room in a frenzy, tearing things apart, searching every desk. Linda followed my lead but was far more careful than I was. This was, after all, a teacher's room.

Kelly and the girls joined me.

"I couldn't stop them," Kelly said. "They wanted to help."

If I'd been a responsible adult in my right mind, I probably would've sent them back out. But I wanted to find Rex. I knew there was another clue yet. But maybe this one would lead us to Rex sooner. I could use the help.

Kelly ordered the girls to follow my path of destruction and in my wake put things back where they were supposed to be. In the distance I heard a siren.

"I called Officer Weir," Kelly said when she saw that I'd noticed. "I thought this was easier than us getting arrested for breaking into the school."

I gave her a quick nod. No matter what I did, Kelly would always be more responsible than me. I'd have to live with that. Besides, I didn't want the girls to have breaking and entering on their records at age ten.

"Ms. Wrath?" Ted Weir and Kevin Dooley walked into the room, but I didn't respond because I found what I was looking for.

There, on one of the bulletin boards, was a cell phone. It was Rex's.

And that was when I heard the lyrics of the music playing on a cassette in a radio on the desk:

*It doesn't matter if you have millions of dollars or a single dime...*

*Because all of us are living on borrowed time...*

I didn't recognize the song, but then, I didn't listen to the radio much. The song had to be a clue. It could wait. The cell was the most important clue here. Without asking, I reached over and pulled a pair of rubber gloves from Ted Weir's utility belt and put them on. Then I gingerly removed the tape from Rex's phone and looked it over.

"Do you know the password?" Ted asked. He didn't seem upset. He obviously wanted Rex back also.

I nodded. "Yes, but I have to take off my gloves to do it. I think you should brush it for fingerprints first."

Because I was wearing his pair, Officer Weir took Kevin's gloves from his belt. Kevin just stood there like he expected Ted to do that. I handed the policeman the phone.

He squinted at it. "The clue sent you here?"

Linda stepped up and showed him the puzzle, but I was lost in thought. Why put the phone here in the school? Why not in my house or something like that? And what was up with the song about borrowed time?

"Something's wrong," I said at last. "The kidnapper is telling us something different."

"What do you mean?" Kelly asked.

"He or she took Rex. Then took Juliette. They aren't beyond hurting people close to me."

Kelly looked stricken. Linda and Ted frowned. The little girls were staring at me with hopeful, shining eyes. Kevin was going through the teacher's candy jar.

"They sent us here because they know this is where the troop meets," I said slowly. "I think the girls might be the next target."

Before we could stop them, Betty walked over to the chalkboard and grabbed the pointer stick and began spinning it like a martial arts fighting staff. Lauren started weaving a bullwhip with rope from the blinds, and Inez broke a small wooden stool and handed the broken legs to the Kaitlyns.

Betty jumped up on the teacher's desk and shouted, "Let them come! There's still one dwarf in Moria who still draws breath!"

"What did she say?" Ted asked.

"Someone's been watching *Lord of the Rings*." I sighed and held my hands up. "Hold on, ladies! Stop arming yourselves! It's just a theory!"

Officer Weir insisted we leave as he gently collected the makeshift weapons, and I left a note telling the teacher I'd replace the stool. Kelly gathered up the girls, and Linda helped get them into the two vans. I shut off the lights and followed the policemen out of the building.

Ted pulled the door shut, and I heard a satisfying snick, indicating it had locked.

"What do you think?" he asked me.

"I have no idea," I answered. "Maybe Rex's cell has something on it?" Should I touch it? If there were fingerprints on it, that might be the quickest way to find this guy. On the other hand, the kidnapper might have wiped it clean.

"It may not," the officer said. "That may be all the kidnapper intended. To prove he has Rex. Kind of like a proof of life." He looked back at the door. "I'll call the sheriff to come over with his team to check the place out. I'll come here before school starts and question the teacher and inform the principal."

Ted was a good cop with a tough job. I felt a twinge in my stomach. It was time to come clean. "I have something else to tell you. And you're probably not going to like it."

His eyebrows went up, and I told him about the conversation I recorded at Vy Todd's house.

"All three of them were there, and they were up to something," I stressed.

The policeman sighed a sigh I was well acquainted with after years of getting involved in cases that weren't mine. I wished that it was Rex sighing at me in frustration. We had to find him, and soon. Too much longer and bad things would happen. I just knew it. Time was not on our side when someone sinister was calling the shots.

Ted looked puzzled. "If you're right, and Vy Todd is behind this, your troop may have tipped their hand. That's why they used the school."

I really didn't want to hear that.

"I don't like this." He frowned. "When it was just you, sure, you've had experience and can take care of yourself. But these little girls…"

"Did you not see them making weapons just now?" I asked. "Lauren booby traps her bedroom, and Betty is lethal. I don't know how, but I just know she is."

"Still." Ted wasn't giving up. "This is getting bad."

I threw my hands up in frustration. "It already was bad when Rex was kidnapped!"

We stared at each other for a minute or two.

"Send me the recording," he said finally. "Immediately. And get those girls home. Tomorrow, I'd like to meet with you,

Mrs. Albers, Linda, and Mr. Andrews. We're going to have to hammer out some rules."

I agreed.

As Kelly and I drove to the end of the block to my house, several cars filled with parents staring at cell phones waited for us. My co-leader unloaded the girls and left to take Linda home.

"Keep this to yourselves," I said quietly to the girls before letting them go. "And keep an eye out for anything dangerous. If you see something, call me immediately."

"Should we kill them first?" Caterina asked.

"Hog-tie them," Lauren insisted. "That way we can interrogate them." She slammed her fist into her open palm.

"Don't do anything! Just call me!"

Once they pinky swore to agree (there are very few things that can break a pinky-swear promise), I released them. Kelly texted that she was heading home to check on Robert and Finn. When the last car pulled away, I walked across the street to Rex's house.

"Mrs. Wrath?" Bart answered the door. "How much longer do you need me?"

I sighed. "Have your mom bring a bunch of clothes. This might take a while."

The kid went back to the couch, where I noticed the two cats and dog were waiting to turn him into a pillow. If my pets were upset about me being gone so long, they didn't show it.

Was Bart in trouble? Juliette had broken in here. Granted, she was on an errand from the evil twin future sister-in-law, but would the killer come here too? Bart was sitting in front of the TV, playing a video game.

"Um, Bart?" I sat down next to him.

Philby and Martini came over and sniffed me before moving to the other side of the boy. They were shaming me for leaving them. I'd been through this before. And I had no time to worry about their feelings.

"Yeah?" the kid asked without looking up from the TV.

"I don't know what you've heard," I said slowly, "but you might be in danger here. I'm investigating Detective Ferguson's kidnapping and…"

"Yup," he said. "I know all about that."

"Are you okay with staying here alone?" I had to ask. Even though he was a teenager, he was still a kid. And I was responsible for him too.

"No problem." Again, his eyes were glued to the game. "Betty made me a zip gun and some booby traps. I'll put them out after you leave."

Of course she did.

Back at my house, I sent Ted the audio, texted the others to meet at the police station in the morning, and headed to bed. One more night without Rex. It was the sixth day since my fiancé had gone missing, and I was only a bit closer to solving this. At least it looked more like Rex's old enemies were involved since I hadn't seen hide nor hair of Lana and Leiko.

If they knew about Rex, it made sense, I guess, that they knew about Juliette. But how did they know about my troop? These guys must've been watching me for some time. Enough to know about the wedding and my meetings, among other things.

I needed to take this into my own hands. Oh, I'd meet with everyone tomorrow. But after that, I was going after Vy Todd and the others. If it was the last thing I did.

# CHAPTER FOURTEEN

————

Riley was standing on my doorstep first thing in the morning as I opened the front door to leave.

"Do you have a minute?" he asked as he pushed past me into my house.

As much as this was an intrusion, it wasn't a surprise. Riley always just walked into my house. It drove me nuts, but short of killing him, there wasn't much I could do about it. I followed him to the breakfast bar and sat down.

He seemed nervous, agitated. That was unusual. Riley was usually confident and in control. What was going on?

"Talk," I said. I wasn't wasting any more time.

"Leiko has turned up in Tokyo," he said, "But no one has seen Lana…really seen Lana for several days." He held up a map of the world, covered in sharpie Xs. "Her tracker is going crazy. She'll be in two cities in separate hemispheres in a matter of a couple of hours."

I stared at the map. Lana appeared to have been in every city in the world, except…

"The only country not marked up is the US," I said.

He nodded. "And that's why I think she's here."

I took this in and let it roll around in my head like a loose marble. "No sightings here at all?"

He shook his head in a way that told me he really didn't want to shake his head.

"It can't be her. I heard Vy Todd, Harvey Oak, and Prescott Winters III talking yesterday. It has to be them." I told him the whole story of the troop outing. He smiled at Betty's ingenuity. He listened carefully when I played the recording.

"To me," Riley said, "it sounds like they are just starting to plan something. It doesn't sound like they've already done it."

I nodded. "Unless Vy started it and realized she needed help, so she brought these two in. Otherwise, they have no connection except for being arrested by Rex."

"There could be another connection we don't know about," Riley said.

"You mean like Vy's connection to you?" I snapped. It was unfair, I supposed, but I was so over this. I just wanted Rex home, safe. Oh yeah, and Juliette too, I guess.

"Right," Riley said. "I get that. I'd probably feel the same way. It would explain how she knew where I was living. But what's the connection to Bobby Ray? How would Vy know that he was your replacement? You're connected to the Agency, and you didn't know that."

He made sense. "That's a good point. Every time it looks like this is about me, it changes to look like it's about Rex."

"Let me ask you something that you may not have thought of," Riley said. "Is it possible that you and Rex were connected before you moved back here?"

My jaw dropped. "Of course not! How could we have known each other before? I only met him when he moved in across the street and had to investigate me in the death of Carlos the Armadillo!" That was a case of the drug cartel leader flying into the road and hitting my car, which means it wasn't my fault. And I got a hottie boyfriend out of it, so it was a win-win.

"You didn't know Rex had been in Davenport before he moved here. You didn't know he'd been involved in a couple of very high-profile investigations."

"Exactly! I didn't know him then. You're proving my point."

He shook his head, "What I'm establishing is that you really don't know much about your fiancé before you met him. Doesn't that also mean you two could've crossed paths before? Or that you were connected in your past?"

"Let me get this straight—you think this is someone who knows both of us? Who blames us for something that happened a long time ago, something we were both involved in? That's crazy."

"It's the only thing that makes sense."

I shook my head. "It doesn't make sense at all. I worked in places like Chechnya, Japan, Colombia, Russia. CIA doesn't work stateside. Rex has only worked here. There's no way we crossed paths somewhere. I'd remember!"

"Alright." Riley held his hands up. "It's just an idea. That's all. Don't get angry."

I glared at him. "Let's go. The police are waiting for us."

\* \* \*

"I wanted to talk to everyone," Officer Ted Weir said as he stood and the rest of us sat.

We were all sitting around a conference room table, waiting to be chastised. At least, I was. I wasn't sure about everyone else. The only unexpected addition was Sheriff Carnack, who didn't sit at the table but instead filled up a seat in the corner.

"I know we all agreed to work together on this," Weir continued. "And I know that's unusual from the way Detective Ferguson handled things."

It was unusual. This would be about the time Rex asked me not to interfere in an investigation for the fortieth time. I missed that.

"But things are getting a little out of hand." As much as he tried not to look at me, I knew he meant me. "We have to keep each other informed. I need to be made aware of everything going on"—now he did look at me—"before we involve little girls in spying on murderers. Before we find a body at someone else's residence."

He had a point. But I was in a hurry. I had very little time to waste. We were now on day seven of Rex's disappearance. I was anxious that we were running out of time. Borrowed time. And there'd been no additional crossword at the site of the last clue. We had one more left. Blue. I was worried now that we'd be too late.

"What about Rex's cell?"

Ted shook his head. "No prints. One of the deputies hacked into it. There's nothing on there after he was kidnapped. It was just a proof of life. This guy wants to spook you."

I didn't respond, because I agreed.

"I've filled Sheriff Carnack in." He nodded to the large man, who nodded back. "And he wants me to keep working on this."

The meth ring in Bladdersly must be giving him fits. Carnack was doing us a favor by not taking over the case—that allowed me to investigate. I owed the big man one. Maybe when this was over and I got Rex back, I could do a little undercover work for him. Or give him Girl Scout Cookies. Or both.

"Here's what we know." Ted went to a dry erase board and started writing down the list of our potential suspects. He included Lana and Leiko. I gave Riley a sideways glance, but he appeared to be engrossed in the proceedings. My former handler had told the police about his suspicions. I didn't like it. Especially since I now didn't think Lana or Leiko were involved.

As Ted rehashed the murders of Spitz and Pratt, his voice trailed off in my head.

On the other hand, what if Riley was right? What if Vy knew about a connection between Rex and me before? Lana knew both of us because she'd stayed with me about the time I'd met Rex. She also knew about my troop. She might even know who replaced me at Langley. But had she been around long enough to surveil me without me noticing?

I'm a pretty observant person. Part of my spy training was to notice everything around me, from the eye color of the guy who was staring at me to where all the exits were. It made me good at my job.

Had I lost my touch? Was it possible that I'd missed seeing Lana around town? I didn't think so. No, if she'd been in Who's There, I'd have known it. The woman was ridiculously gorgeous. I'd just need to follow the trail of stunned men in her wake. I'd seen men faint around her. Someone like that stood out, a huge no-no in espionage.

Over the years, I was sure my success was due to the fact that I was so ordinary. Average height, build, with forgettable features. Anonymity was the best tool in my kit. Well, and knife throwing. I was very good at knife throwing.

But, now that I knew what Vy Todd, Harvey Oak, and Prescott Winters III looked like, had I seen them around town before Rex was kidnapped? It seemed impossible that he wouldn't notice them right away since he'd arrested them.

Who was I kidding? This whole case was impossible.

Kelly elbowed me hard in the ribs. "Pay attention!"

That was when I realized that there was one more name on the board under the list of suspects.

Mine.

I raised my hand. "Um, why am I up there?"

Ted realized I hadn't heard whatever explanation he'd just given.

*Ahem.* He cleared his throat. "In 99 percent of these kinds of cases, it's usually the spouse who commits the crime."

"I'm a suspect?" I roared as I got to my feet.

"He's just looking at it from all possible angles," Kelly said. "You weren't listening."

Weir nodded vigorously. "I've put everything on the board that is a possibility."

That was when I realized there was a lot on the board that wasn't there before. Next to my name was an idea for Rex running away, driving his car off a cliff in an extremely rural area, and the last one just said *Twister.*

"We don't get many tornados in December," I grumbled as I sat back down.

"I don't think you are responsible for Detective Ferguson's disappearance," Ted said with a sigh. "I just have to include everything so I can rule things out."

I asked, "What about Juliette Dowd? What did you find at her house?"

He shook his head. "Nothing. Not so much as a fingerprint. Her car was found at the Girl Scout Council office, but she wasn't there. In fact, she hadn't been there in days."

"You should put her name up there," I said. "She could've taken Rex and run off when things got too hot." It would be really nice if Juliette was the killer/kidnapper. I knew I could take her.

Ted actually wrote her name under suspects. Huh. He really was doing what he said.

"What about the postmortems on the two victims?" Linda asked.

I hadn't thought of that. It was a good thing I had her. I gave her a thumbs-up, and she gave me that smile I'd loved so much as a kid in her class. It made me feel a little better.

"Mr. Spitz was stabbed through the heart. Bobby Ray Pratt was strangled. Nothing more. Both cases were pretty cut and dried as far as how they died."

Officer Kevin Dooley walked into the room. He looked at me before handing Ted Weir a file. There was a weird look in his eye as he walked out. Maybe because for the first time since I'd known him, he wasn't eating. I had a bad feeling about this.

Ted looked through the file then turned his eyes on me.

"Can I talk to you," he said to me, "in my office?"

I looked around. Every head swiveled toward me.

"Sure," I said as breezily as possible. I didn't feel that way inside. I had that feeling you get when you're busted for something you don't remember doing, which is the *worst*.

I followed Officer Weir to Rex's office, a little put out that he called it his. He sat at Rex's desk, and I sat in the chair across from him.

"Ms. Wrath," he said in a hollow tone. "Is there anything you want to tell me?"

Was there? I couldn't think of anything. In fact, I'd been pretty good with sharing what I knew with him. Okay, so sometimes it was later than usual, but I did share.

"No," I answered.

He looked at the file and then at me. Leaning back in Rex's chair, he fixed a stern gaze on me. He might be a newbie, but he was learning fast. I started to sweat.

"I've just received some information that incriminates you in the disappearance of Detective Ferguson."

"You what?" My jaw dropped. "There isn't anything that incriminates me, because I didn't do it!"

Ted chewed his lip. Then he checked his watch. He didn't talk at all. It was a good interrogation technique. I'd used it myself to great success. Stare someone down long enough and they will talk to fill the uncomfortable silence.

I took a different approach. I glared back at him. "You'd better tell me what's going on."

He leaned back and folded his arms over his chest. Apparently he got an *A* in intimidation at the Academy. I didn't care. If he didn't tell me what was in that file, I was going to take it from him and read it myself.

"Oh no!" I gasped and pointed out the window behind him. "What's that?"

He turned to look, and I snatched the file folder.

"You tricked me!" he cried.

My eyes were scanning the contents of the file. "Yeah, I don't know how you fell for that."

There was one sheet of paper. It was a typed letter in a baggie. An anonymous note that said I kidnapped and killed Detective Rex Ferguson. I tried to dampen my outrage as I forced myself to read:

*Merry Wrath kidnapped and killed her fiancé, Detective Ferguson. He discovered a criminal element in her past that would send her to prison. She had to get him out of the way. I saw her do this, and I have proof.*

The letter then went on to say some rather unkind things about my physical features and insult my cats. They didn't need to say that, as the damage had been done in the first sentence. I sucked in a breath. Was Rex dead, or was that just another lie? It had to be. I couldn't go on if I thought that was true.

I leveled my gaze at the rookie. "You aren't seriously buying this, are you? It's an anonymous note, for crying out loud."

Ted's eyes faltered for a moment then recovered. "We have to look into every clue, Ms. Wrath." He nodded at the letter. "And that includes anonymous letters."

"It's a crank letter, a red herring trying to get you off track," I snapped. "What about real proof, like the cabal meeting I recorded at Vy Todd's house?"

"We're looking into that too. The Des Moines police are managing a stakeout. If something is going on, we'll find it."

I narrowed my gaze. "And Rex. You'll find Rex."

He sighed. "I'm sorry, Ms. Wrath. But I think it's time to remove you from the investigation."

"Why?" I finally get to investigate, and I get yanked from that?

"Because you are a suspect!"

My eyes dropped to a pen set on the desk. If I wanted to, I could kill Officer Ted Weir four different ways with those pens. But then the suspicion against me would be justified. And if I was kicked off the official investigation, I could do it on my own. And I wouldn't have to report every move to the police.

It was just that I was really excited about being officially involved for once.

"Fine," I said at last. "What happens now?"

"You leave, and I go and tell the team what happened."

Considering that they were my team, I was pretty sure it wouldn't go down well. I got up from my chair and grabbed my coat, shrugging it on as I made my little walk of shame through the station.

Kevin Dooley was dumping half a box of sugar into one cup of coffee as I walked past. He gave me a look that I couldn't interpret, but if I had to guess, it would be a smug one.

"Go to hell, Kevin," I grumbled before walking out the door.

I drove to Riley's office, used my lockpicks to break in, and sat on the couch. Since it might be a few moments, I decided to follow up on his bizarre theory about Rex and me having a previous connection.

"Hey, kiddo," Mom answered on the first ring. "Any news?"

"None yet." My voice cracked a little. "I have a question. Can you patch Dad in?"

"Of course! Just a moment," Mom said, and the line went quiet as she went to get him on speaker phone.

"Hey, Merry." Dad's voice was full of sympathy. "What can we do to help?"

I wondered why Riley wasn't pulling up to the office in outrage of what he'd just heard. Maybe he had Ted in a headlock. The thought made me smile, but I went on with my query.

"Have you guys ever met the Fergusons before?" I thought about what Riley said about Rex's and my paths crossing, and started with familial connections. "Maybe you'd met them years ago?" Hopefully it wasn't that we were related somehow.

My parents acted as if this was the most normal question ever. "No, I'm sure we haven't," Mom answered.

"I'd remember them," Dad said. "But your mother's memory is way better than mine. So if she says we've never seen them before we met them officially, then we never met them."

He was right. Mom had a near photographic memory when it came to people. Which was why she was so good at being a senator's wife. She could mix and mingle with anyone and remember their name the next time she saw them, whether a month or a decade later.

"Okay. Just trying to debunk a line of questioning." I promised to call them the minute I knew anything, gave them my love, and hung up.

The parking lot was still empty. Where was Riley? Had he drunk the Kool-Aid and bought the idea that I was involved? Didn't seem likely. Riley knew me longer than anyone in that room, save for Kelly.

And why wasn't my cell going off like mad? If they weren't here, they should at least be texting me to say how insane the accusation was. They didn't believe an anonymous letter. Did they?

This was a huge mess. I wanted to go home, eat a gallon of ice cream, wash it down with my tears, and check out. But I couldn't do that. Rex was counting on me to rescue him. I *knew* he was still alive. And I knew I wasn't the one who took him.

The anonymous letter could be a crank or from the kidnapper. Rex told me they get crazy leads all the time from the public. Some people try to capitalize on a case because they are lonely and need attention or because they are mean-spirited, and in some cases, downright nuts.

If this was the kidnapper, why would they say I kidnapped and killed Rex? My stomach dropped, and I shuddered.

They killed Lewis Spitz and Bobby Ray Pratt. What did the murderer stand to gain by killing Rex also?

I needed to find Rex and now.

I sat down at Riley's computer and started it up. A password prompt was easy to bypass. Riley always used the same password, *LadiesMan#1*. He never changed it. It drove the CIA's IT department crazy, but the man refused to come up with a new password (and to be honest, it wasn't that original). I typed it in, and we were off and running.

The main screen had several icons, and it took me a moment to make sense of them. *Open* meant an ongoing investigation. And *Done* meant the case was closed. *Possiblities* did not refer to cases—it referred to women. Sometimes the man was far too predictable.

I clicked on *Open*, and because he didn't have any cases, there was only one icon with my name on it. He hadn't progressed very far in getting answers. I found some emails sent to his contacts at the Agency, but no one had found anything out yet. He'd even queried the FBI, but they didn't even respond.

After leaving the CIA, Riley worked for the Feds, briefly. There was very little love lost between our two branches, and since he wasn't a lifer, the FBI wouldn't cough up any resources. I wasn't at all surprised that they hadn't answered his call for action.

And where was Riley? I checked my cell. Nothing. No one who'd been at the meeting had called, texted, or at least stormed out in outrage over the accusation leveled against me. I was sure my friends didn't believe it. So where were they?

I was the only one Rex could really count on. The police were useless in this matter if they believed random notes from anonymous sources. My family had gone home (at my urging), and my friends had other things to deal with in their daily lives.

If I was on my own, I could handle it. In the field it had just been me and Riley, and in many cases where there was complete radio silence, just me. I was used to working alone. Over the past few years, I'd gotten a little rusty. But once a spy, always a spy.

Okay, so no one ever says that. I just made it up.

Should I text everyone and ask what was going on? It didn't seem right that I should have to do that. They should be on my side. At any rate, the complete silence told me all I needed to know. The only way to find Rex was on my own. I just needed a place to start.

Movement in the lower right-hand corner of Riley's screen caught my attention. I clicked on the icon that was labeled *WebCam*. There were several icons, including the school, both grocery stores, and the zoo. Only one was open to reveal a hidden camera outside the one gas station in town. Why was Riley watching that place?

I guess it made sense. We were half an hour from the big city. Almost everyone who came out here had to stop there to get gas or something to eat or drink. People often assume that because of the anonymity, gas stations and convenience stores are good places to use to hide out.

The truth was exactly the opposite. Most gas stations and convenience stores had security cameras. They were the main defense against idiots who thought they would be getting away with something. Plus, I always suspected that the staff looked over the recordings when they were bored.

The image was in black and white and slightly grainy. A woman was pumping gas, her back toward me. There was something familiar about her. Leaning closer to the screen, I studied her, but she didn't turn my way.

She wore her hair in a short, dark bob, and the bulky winter coat gave me no idea of her figure. And yet, I could swear I'd seen her before. Finally, she went into the gas station. I waited a few minutes, tearing through my memories, thinking about her mannerisms, stance, and so on, but came up with nothing.

The gas station door opened, and the woman walked toward her car and the camera. She kept her eyes downcast, but at the last second, she looked up straight into the camera. The woman broke into an evil grin. I knew that grin.

Lana winked at me before she climbed into the black SUV and drove away.

# CHAPTER FIFTEEN

———

I ran out the door and jumped into my van, roaring out of the lot. The gas station was on the other end of town, but considering that everything in Who's There is five minutes away, I could make it there in three. Two if the roads were empty.

The tires on my van squealed as I made a sharp turn onto Main Street. Lana had a few minutes' lead on me, but the way that she grinned at the camera told me she wanted me to know she was here. She had to know I'd follow her.

Which probably meant a trap. And if I wasn't so out of my mind with fear and fury, I might've been a bit more cautious. But it had been seven days since Rex disappeared. And I wasn't taking any chances of losing her.

I hit the gas station in two minutes, shaving time off of my personal best. I pulled in where she'd been and then drove off in the direction I'd seen her go. There were only two ways out of town, and she was on one of them, unless she doubled back.

However, if she'd taken the obvious road, she'd be on her way to Des Moines by now. I had to take that chance if I wanted to catch her. Roaring through town, going 50 mph in a 20-mph zone, I dodged a squirrel crossing the street and got an angry fist shaking from a farmer driving a tractor.

I was on the narrow two-lane road that would take me to the interstate. Just a few hundred feet more and I...

*Crash!*

The nose end of a car blew through my passenger door before disengaging. The van started to spin, and I wondered if I'd put on my seat belt in my rush to catch Lana. I decided that I had when I didn't go flying through the windshield. The airbag deployed, and the last thing I remembered was catching a glimpse of a damaged black SUV as my world went black.

* * *

I was dreaming. I had to be, because as far as I knew, they didn't make six-foot-tall Pizza Rolls. I was chasing them with a vat of ranch dressing, but they were too fast, which was strange since they didn't seem to have legs or feet.

I had almost caught one and reached out to touch it when it dissolved completely. Now I was on a gravel road in the country, walking toward an intersection.

I'd just about reached it when I saw someone coming toward me. It was a man with dark hair. He smiled as he drew near. It was Rex! I wanted to run and jump into his arms, but for some reason I froze, unable to move.

Rex said nothing more. It was as if he didn't know me. He strode through the intersection, nodded at me, and kept going. My feet finally started moving, but in the other direction. I tried screaming, but nothing came out. I walked through the intersection and kept travelling on my own road as Rex walked off into the sunset.

Then Philby, who'd grown to giant proportions and now resembled a Hitler-like five-story building, loomed over me. She scooped me up with her paw and brought me to her mouth. She opened wide and tossed me down her throat into total darkness.

"No!" I sat straight up.

There was no cat, no roads, just a nondescript room that smelled like antiseptic. I turned to look around and felt a crushing pain in my neck.

"It's okay," a soothing male voice said. "You're alright."

In spite of the pain, I turned my whole body to see Riley sitting in a chair next to my hospital bed.

"What happened?" was all I could think to say.

"You were in a car accident," my former handler said. "Hit and run. The police are out looking for the other car."

I rubbed the back of my neck. "They won't find her."

Riley cocked his head to the side. "Her? You know who did this?"

I wanted to nod. I really did. But it hurt.

"Hey!" I said. "You know what?"

Riley asked, "What?"

"Come closer," I said. "I can't see or hear very well."

Riley got up and leaned over me. With all the strength I could muster, I went to slap him in the face but ended up hitting his shoulder.

"You didn't stand up for me!"

He sat back down and looked confused. "What are you talking about?"

"Officer Weir! And that completely baseless accusation that I'd kidnapped and killed Rex!" I flinched at the sound of my voice. Even sound hurt. "You didn't storm out of there in indignation!"

"Wrath," he said as he patted my arm. "No one bought that. We spent half an hour arguing with Ted about it. Your Linda put up one hell of a fight."

"And?"

"He's agreed...to an extent." He held up his hands. "You're still a suspect, but at the very bottom of the list."

"I'm still a suspect?" I screamed. It came out more like the sound a strangled chicken makes.

"Hardly at all," he reassured. "What happened? Where did you go?"

"Back to your office. By the way, you should get better locks. I called Mom to see if we had any connection to the Fergusons before I met Rex."

"My theory." Riley grinned. "You took it seriously!"

"No. I just wanted to eliminate it. That's all," I grumbled.

"Then what? You weren't at the office when I got there, and the next thing I'd heard, you were in that accident."

I struggled to sit up, and he stuffed a pillow behind my back. That was nice.

"It was no accident. I got onto your computer and saw the security camera at the gas station. I saw Lana."

Riley's eyes grew wide. "You saw her?"

I really wanted to nod but decided against it. "She had short hair and a big coat, but it was her. She looked right into the camera and smiled. I took off to find her. And she ambushed me."

He actually gasped. "Lana is the one who hit you?"

"It has to be. It explains why she didn't stick around."

Riley frowned. "Why would she want you to see her?"

"Maybe she thought I was moving too slowly on the clues? Although that doesn't make sense because other than Rex's cell, we didn't find a new clue in the classroom."

Talking was taking a lot out of me. I slumped against the pillow and took a couple of deep breaths. I hadn't been in this much pain since I fell out of a tree a few months ago and hit every branch on the way down.

"Why were you watching that place?" I croaked.

He shrugged. "It's the most obvious spot in town. Everyone stops there at one time or another."

Of course he knew that. If I knew that, Riley knew that.

He got up and closed the door. "You really think you saw her?"

I narrowed my eyes. "What do you mean, 'think'? Of course I saw her! Go get the footage from the gas station!"

"I don't have to. I'm recording the footage from all of my hidden cameras," Riley said as a nurse came in and injected something into my IV.

"No more drugs," I complained weakly.

The nurse fluffed my pillow. "I promised Kelly Albers that I'd make sure you rest."

"You're friends with Kelly?"

The woman nodded. "We went to nursing school together. I'm Joyce."

She left, and I felt wobbly. The room wiggled menacingly.

Riley got to his feet. "Sleep it off. I'll be back. I just need to get that footage. See you soon." He kissed my forehead, but I was too weak to complain. Seconds later, I lost consciousness.

\* \* \*

I was dreaming again. I was in an all-black room. In the center of the room, about one hundred yards away, was a trumpet on a table. Rex appeared out of nowhere...walked up to the trumpet and played it. Huh. I didn't know he could do that. I started walking toward him, but when I was still a couple of yards away, he set it down and, giving me a polite smile, vanished into thin air.

I walked over to the trumpet and picked it up. In my whole life I'd never played an instrument, but I put the trumpet to my lips and played a piece of classical music. Then I set the trumpet down and walked away in another direction.

My eyes fluttered open. No Rex. I was still in the hospital room. How long had I been out?

"You've been asleep for a whole day," Joyce the nurse said.

"Did Kelly have you drug me again?" This would be the third time in a week that my friend ordered my doping. I really should have a conversation with her about that.

"She talked to the doctor about it, and he ordered it," she said. "How are you feeling?"

I sat up a bit easier. I'd always been a quick healer.

"Better. Has anyone been by?"

Joyce looked like she'd rather not answer. She looked toward the closed door.

"What?" I asked, my spy-dy senses tingling.

"You have a policeman standing guard," she said.

Great. "Was that Kelly's idea too?" I grumbled.

The nurse shook her head. "No. They just showed up yesterday and change shifts every so often."

I thought for a moment. "Who's out there now?"

Joyce walked out of the room. Five minutes later, she appeared with a covered tray, which she set down on the table. I pulled the lid off, ravenously hungry. It didn't look half-bad. Soup and bread. I wolfed it down.

"It says *Dooley* on his name tag," Joyce said quietly.

At last! A glimmer of hope!

The nurse smiled and walked out of the room.

Police surveillance, huh? Had something happened that made me a prime suspect, or were they protecting me from Lana? I really needed to know what was going on, but my cell was nowhere to be found. I polished off the soup and bread, closed my eyes, and thought things through.

"Hey." Riley stuck his head through the door. "You're up." He walked in and set a paper bag on the table in front of me. "I thought you could use these."

Oreos! I tore into them, eating a whole row until I started to feel like my old self.

"Thank you!" I leaned back against the bed. "I needed that."

Riley laughed. "It looks that way."

"Tell me something," I licked the crumbs from my lips. "Why is there a policeman outside?"

He leaned forward. "They think you were making a getaway attempt when you got hit."

"You have to be kidding me! I'm still a suspect?"

The man shrugged. "They don't believe the story about Lana."

"But you have the proof! You have a camera at the gas station! You have the footage!"

Riley said nothing for a moment.

"Tell me you got it," I growled.

"I got it." He looked at the door then back at me. "But honestly, it doesn't look like Lana to me."

"How can you say that?" My jaw dropped open. "It's totally Lana! Just different hair!"

Riley shrugged. "I guess it could be, but the woman didn't look like her to me. It was kind of grainy."

I know what I saw. "Did you get the license plate number?"

He shook his head. "Obscured by snow."

What was happening? Was I losing my mind? I knew that was Lana. Didn't I?

"What do you want to do?" Riley asked.

I thought for a moment before sitting up and swinging my legs over the side of the bed. "Give me your cell. I don't know where mine is."

To my surprise, he handed over *my* cell.

I snatched it from his grip. "Why did you have this?"

"The police were looking for it. Said they needed to check it out."

He was on my side. "Thanks for taking it. Do they really have something on me?"

Riley scooted his chair closer. "I did a little flirting with the dispatcher at the station."

Of course he did. Riley could melt the panties off of Margaret Thatcher.

"She took a look at the board. Carnack and Ted moved you up, even with Vy Todd. She said they found a strange shopping list in your car."

They might've had me there. I was a list maker. I made lists of everything, and my van was littered with them because I never cleaned it out. But I was pretty sure there was a list in there that had duct tape, zip ties, and a ski mask because the girls wanted to know how to escape being kidnapped. Kelly voted it down in the end, but I'd thought about holding on to it for the right moment.

"Dammit. I didn't give permission to search my car."

"You didn't need to. Kelly did. She didn't think you had anything in there that would incriminate you."

Kelly should've known better. And we were going to have a little talk when this was over.

"So after I get better, it's off to interrogation, I guess." I hit speed dial. When there was an answer on the other end, I ordered a large deep-dish pepperoni pizza to be delivered to my room. I gave them a credit card number to pay for it. "It's for Officer Kevin Dooley."

The guy promised it would be here in twenty minutes. That should be plenty of time.

"I'll need your coat and hat," I said to Riley.

"You're going to run?" His expression said that he didn't think that was a good idea.

I stepped onto the floor. There was still a lot of pain, but at this point I could handle it. Riley retrieved the paper bag with my clothes for me. They were clean and folded. That had to be Kelly. Maybe I'd go a little easy on her.

It took ten minutes to get dressed. Riley stood in the corner like a naughty boy until I told him he could turn around.

Sitting back on the bed, I steeled myself for what I had to do next.

"Pizza should be delivered to Kevin in a few minutes," I warned. "You need to either be me or stuff the pillows under the covers to look like me."

"Where are you going to go? Out the window?" He looked incredulous. "Doesn't that seem a bit dangerous in your condition? Besides, they took your keys. All of them."

I rolled my eyes. "We're on the first floor." I hobbled over to the window and unlocked it. There'd be a five-foot drop from the window, but that was nothing compared to being hit by a car.

"What should I do?" Riley whispered.

Opening the window, I straddled the sash. "If you're not going to get in the bed, you just walk out the way you came. Kevin will be in a pizza-induced coma soon. He won't even notice that you're not wearing a coat."

Gauging the drop, I grabbed my purse and phone and fell to the ground outside. I didn't stop until I was a good four blocks away. Every muscle in my body screamed at me, but I needed to have a normal gait to avoid suspicion from passersby, so I pushed through it.

First things first, I needed to get to my house before the hospital knew I was gone. Then I needed transportation and a safe house. That would be harder to come by in Who's There, but I'd figure something out. Maybe I could live in Betty's closet. I was fairly certain that girl could be trusted.

The cold helped with the pain as I walked calmly to my house, zigzagging in between alleys and streets. It took longer than I thought to get there, but I managed to arrive at my back door in fifteen minutes.

You might think that breaking into your own house is easy. And you'd be right because I always left a key in a can of ant poison next to a dozen dead carpenter ants (I took a cue from the twins' taxidermy dioramas) on the back deck. It didn't take long to get into the garage and my house.

There was very little time to organize my getaway. It was broad daylight, so at least I didn't need the lights on. I filled a duffel bag with a ghost chip for my cell, nonperishable food (aka junk food that wouldn't expire until the next decade), bottles of water, my laptop, cell charger, a couple of changes of clothes, a few spy trifles, and my gun with two extra magazines.

As I walked through the kitchen, I spotted a picture of Rex and me on the fridge. Kelly always tried to take me shopping for picture frames, but magnets are just as good, right?

Rex gave me an amused grin as I sat next to him on a picnic table bench, talking animatedly. I could almost feel the weight of his arm around my shoulders and the warmth from his body. We'd been at a cookout at Kelly's, and someone took that picture. I ran my thumb over his face as tears pricked my eyelids.

"I'm going to find you," I whispered. "And I'm not waiting one more minute to do it."

# CHAPTER SIXTEEN

———

I crossed the street and went into Rex's house. Bart was asleep on the sofa with the two cats and dog on top of him. For a moment I thought maybe I should check to see if he was still alive, but then I thought better of it. He didn't need to know I'd been here.

Rex kept a spare set of keys in the kitchen, and I snagged them and went to the garage. If I was lucky, they hadn't impounded his SUV. Unlucky? Well, I'd have to figure something else out.

Bingo. I dumped my stuff into the front seat, pulled the stocking cap lower on my head, and headed out. The only problem I had was where to go. Like I said, it only took five minutes to get anywhere in this town. Soon I'd hit the country. I needed a place to crash where no one would find me.

I started looking for empty houses for sale. Very few houses were sold in January, so it would be less likely to have a showing. Also, it would be furnished and have power—always a plus.

I drove by a few that were in busy neighborhoods. No good. There were a couple of McMansions on the edge of town, but that wouldn't work since real estate agents probably checked in on the nice properties more regularly to guard their commission.

What about a spot on Main Street? We had a few tall buildings with empty lofts above. It would provide a good vantage spot for watching the comings and goings. But it would be busy too. My bridal store was there, as was a Chinese restaurant and Oleo's, my favorite burger place.

The smell of cooking meat would probably drive me mad with hunger though. And Ferguson Taxidermy was next door, so if Rex's sister Ronni spotted me, she'd report me. No, this wouldn't work at all. Much as I liked the business idea, it would be hard to find a place out of the way that was maybe closed for the season...

That was it! I drove to the edge of town to the perfect place. Parking the car was tricky because if they were looking for Rex's missing car, it might give me away. I pulled into a spot at the hospital and hiked several blocks to the perfect safe house.

\* \* \*

"It's *her* again!" Dickie the scarlet macaw shrieked. Always ready to heckle me, the bird often remembered dialogue muttered by the cranky, awkward teenage boy who cleaned the aviary and fed the birds.

Mr. Fancy Pants, the king vulture, spotted me right away and started pacing in his enclosure. Oh crap. I didn't pack any Girl Scout Cookies. The bird was smitten with Peanut Butter Patties especially and went to great lengths to get them— something I learned when my troop first encountered him in Washington, DC.

He was on loan from the Smithsonian's National Zoo, and I was his sponsor, which meant I paid for his upkeep and broke in regularly to share my troubles with him. He was a very good listener, as long as you brought cookies.

If you've never seen a king vulture before, imagine a cartoon bird with crazy coloring that looked like a schizophrenic toddler painted it. White bodies with black trim, their black and purple bald heads have light stubble on them. The eyes are huge, and sometimes look like they are going in different directions. The beak is topped with a blaze orange wattle. Looking at one brings to mind both astonishment and confusion.

"Nobody ever listens to me, and I have great ideas!" Dickie complained.

I let myself into Fancy Pants' enclosure and sat down on a huge fake branch. The macaw jumped up beside me, eyeing him with his cartoon-like googly eyes. Rummaging through my duffel, I found the Oreos Riley had given me. I really didn't want to share, but the bird wasn't going to be very happy if I didn't give him something. I was like his crack dealer.

Dickie squawked, "My graphic novel has a zombie Pegasus!"

I crushed the Oreos and set them on the branch between us. King vultures have an excellent sense of smell. And Mr. Fancy Pants was no exception. While keeping at least one of his eyes fixed on me, he snatched up a cookie fragment and chewed, or did whatever the equivalent of that was.

"Where's my teddy bear? Where's Sauron?" Dickie said. That was the second *Lord of the Rings* reference in a couple of days.

The Oreos were a hit as Fancy Pants devoured the lot. I crushed a few more and set them between us. The zoo would be the perfect place to stay. Especially the aviary. There was the janitor-kid who also fed the birds once a day. If they were on the same schedule they were this fall, I was good for at least the next fifteen hours.

"I don't know if you've heard," I said quietly, "but Rex is missing. He's been gone a week, and no one knows where he is."

Fancy Pants, finished with the cookies, began to preen his feathers as I told the raptor my sad story.

"Mom!" Dickie squealed. "They're not comic books! They're *collectibles*!"

Either the kid was taking Dickie home with him at night, or he talked to his mother on the phone when he was here. He might be spending too much time here complaining to birds, when he should be trying to deal with the issues that kept girls away from him.

I finished my story, and the tears started to come in an avalanche of emotion. Fancy Pants stopped what he was doing and stared at me. He brought his face closer to mine, eyes on my eyes.

But I couldn't stop. The dam had broken, and the reservoir was emptying out. Everything that had gone wrong exploded in a deluge of sorrow and self-pity. I just let it out, like I had with Riley.

Fancy Pants set his head on my shoulder as I sobbed. It was like a hug, which was nice, or he was thinking I'd die afterward and he'd get dessert. When the tears stopped, I wiped my eyes and turned to see a single feather in his beak. He set it in my hand and put his head back on my shoulder.

"Nobody loves me!" Dickie screamed.

It was getting late, and I made a makeshift bed in a corner of the enclosure. Fancy Pants fell asleep on his branch, and my mind drifted to the dreams I'd had lately. I'd completely ignored them. But it seemed as though my brain was saying that Riley's theory, that Rex and I had a past somehow, was true.

The mind is a strange thing. Sometimes it lies. Was it possible that Riley put that suggestion in my head and my imagination was running amok with it? Or was there a nugget of truth to the idea?

I thought back to my college days at the University of Iowa. Rex once told me he went to Iowa State, so few chances for us to mingle there. After that, I'd joined the CIA and was dispatched all over the world, which made meeting even less likely.

There wasn't any familial connection. At least, Mom and Dad didn't think so. If there was, we would've found it by now. So what was the connection?

And if there was a connection, did that mean the crimes were directed at both of us? Wait…Lana knew both of us when she'd been here before. It would make sense that she knew about us, the girls, and all that. And she was more likely to find my replacement at the CIA than Vy Todd or the others.

Did that mean Lana was the kidnapper and killer?

Something in the back of my mind said there was something else. Riley had suggested we'd met before we'd actually met. But try as I might, I couldn't find the answer there. My dreams made it look like Rex did something before I did…walking to the crossroads, playing trumpet. Whatever our connection, maybe we hadn't met but our paths had intersected.

That was an interesting idea. I pulled out my cell and inserted a ghost chip. That should put off tracking me.

"Merry?" Kelly answered on the first ring. "Where are you? Everyone is looking for you!"

"Are you alone?" I asked.

"I'm giving Finn a bath, so yes, I'm alone," she said with a hint of irritation.

"Do you think it's possible that Rex and I could have crossed paths years before we met?"

"What? How would I know that?" Kelly said, her voice punctuated by the squeals of a happy toddler.

"Riley suggested it. He thinks we are both targeted, and that might be why."

There was silence for a moment. "I'll have to think on that."

"Call me," I warned. "But don't let anyone know I talked to you."

She sighed. "This is crazy. Turn yourself in. You didn't do anything, and eventually they'd figure that out. But going on the run makes you look guilty."

"No. I can't find Rex if I'm locked up. We have one more clue, and I want to be there when it's delivered."

"Then be careful!" Kelly said.

I agreed and hung up. Looking at my watch told me I'd been here for several hours. And I was hungry. Mr. Fancy Pants had eaten all of my Oreos, so I'd have to find something else to eat.

Reaching inside my bag, I felt a can of tuna. Why did I grab that? That was for the cats. Oh well, beggars can't be choosers. I pulled the can out and went to pull the pop tab when I felt something on the bottom.

Taped to the can was a folded sheet of paper. I swallowed hard. Was this the last clue? Very carefully, I pulled it off the can and unfolded it.

*There's no time for a puzzle clue...You'd better be fast to find this Something Blue.*

What did that mean? I read it again. The killer was getting impatient, or they would've created a crossword puzzle. And yet, this was a puzzle, because I had no idea what it meant. The paper itself was some sort of stationary that featured a cabin. Why did the kidnapper change paper? It had to mean something.

And attaching it to the bottom of a tuna tin? Why do that? They must've thought I'd feed the cats and see it.

*You'd better be fast to find this Something Blue.*

Why would something be blue? A chill ran through me. It was winter, so there was the idea that skin turned blue when freezing. Worse yet, if it referred to a living being, that someone outside might die of exposure. I looked at the cabin again. The only cabin I knew about was the one in the middle of town in the park. Owned by the historical society, it would be closed for the season.

I ran all the way to Rex's car and tore off before closing my door. I'd better be wrong about this. It was late at night, which meant I'd be the only car racing through town. That would make me stand out. I'd also have to drive past the police station.

But if I was right, I didn't care if I got caught.

I slowed down a little on Main Street and pulled up to the cabin and parked. There were fresh tracks in the snow. Someone had been here in the last couple of hours. I pulled my coat around me, unsure if I was shivering because it was cold or because I was terrified.

I followed the tracks behind the cabin and spotted a small cage in the snow. Something was inside.

"Philby!" I called out as I ran to the cage, threw the door open, and stuffed one very angry cat into my coat.

*Yeoooow!* My cat screamed at me.

Grabbing the cage, I ran to the car and started it up to get the heater going. My cat was ice cold but probably stayed alive by sheer fury. She was shivering uncontrollably inside my coat as I drove off, using side roads to get to the zoo.

*Yeoooooow!* she chastised.

I couldn't take her home or to Rex's house. The police had most likely found out I'd taken the car. Those two houses would be watched. By the time I pulled up to the zoo, Philby had stopped shivering. Her paws were still cold, but she seemed out of the woods as far as hypothermia was concerned.

I couldn't stay in the car all night. People would notice an unfamiliar car parked and running. Once I was sure Philby was better, I pushed her down into my coat, grabbed the cage, and climbed the fence into the zoo.

There was only one problem. As I entered the aviary, Philby's head popped out of the top of my coat. Her pupils instantly dilated when she saw what she thought was an endless buffet of prey.

Uh-oh.

"No! You can't eat these birds!" I hissed.

Philby was trilling at the birds, which was her way of trying to hypnotize them to climb into her mouth. Usually she did this in the front window where she wasn't a threat. But now, one leap and she'd be free to chase birds as big as her. I didn't know what she was thinking.

I closed my arms around her to hold her in my coat as I advanced to Mr. Fancy Pants' enclosure. What was I doing bringing her here? And why was I taking her to a place where she could trap a bird?

Although Mr. Fancy Pants was bigger than her, my cat had an overly optimistic view of her odds. I sat on the floor in my corner until she was fully warmed up. Then I'd have to put her back into the cage.

She wouldn't like that.

Mr. Fancy Pants hopped over to us, his eyes fixed on the cat who thought she could destroy him. He cocked his head completely to the right side then the left. Then he hopped closer.

Philby was chattering now, convinced she was hypnotizing her prey into lying down and waiting patiently until she could kill and eat him. Mr. Fancy Pants was probably hoping she was dead so he could eat her.

"I don't wanna sort the recyclables!" Dickie shrieked.

At that moment, all hell broke loose. Philby lunged out of my coat toward the vulture, who took off into the air. He landed on a perch about six feet up.

Not to be deterred, Philby scaled the fake branch and started jumping into the air in order to catch her prey.

Mr. Fancy Pants just stared down at her while she bobbed up and down in the air. This was going to end badly. Even though Philby was tough as nails, she was also a possible meal for the raptor.

"Philby! Stop it!" I shouted as I tried to catch the obese cat, who looked like a beach ball with fur on a trampoline.

Mr. Fancy Pants decided enough was enough and flew toward the closed door. He didn't slow down. Did he expect me to open it? I raced to the door and flung it open just before he made contact. That was close.

Philby ran into the main area of the aviary, transfixed by the flying food around her. Little birds chirped loudly, staying as high as they could, while the big birds climbed higher in their enclosures, unaware that they were safe.

"Philby!" I screamed as I ran around like a lunatic, trying to capture a rotund cat who was now miraculously spry.

"Philby!" shouted Dickie. "Philby!"

The cat froze and turned toward the macaw, who was on a perch about four feet off the floor.

"Oh no you don't!" I ran as she ran.

While I didn't like the macaw, I didn't want him to become my cat's dinner either. Dickie sat there, shrieking the cat's name, and I was envious because Philby didn't answer to me. I was almost to the pole when I skidded and fell.

My only hope was that Philby wouldn't be able to jump that high. It was a weak hope, because that cat was capable of anything. That was when I noticed that the feline Hitler wasn't slowing down. I guess once you get bulk like that moving, it's hard to slow down.

I was wrong. Philby connected with the pole, hard, then looked up to receive his prey. Dickie flew and started circling the room, looking like a really expensive cat toy. Meanwhile, Mr. Fancy Pants was sneaking up on Philby.

"Philby! Come here!" I shouted as I crawled toward her.

"Philby! Philby!" Dickie screeched.

The vulture had his wings spread but was running across the floor. This wasn't going to end well. The bird had more weapons than the cat. I had to do something to stop Mr. Fancy Pants.

And then I had it. I waited until Fancy Pants was almost on top of her and shouted, "Bobb!"

Philby closed her eyes and hissed violently, shooting backward like a deflating balloon and skidding into the oncoming raptor. This was a useful tool I'd discovered when Philby moved in. Her previous owner had been named Bobb, with two *b*'s, and he wasn't very nice. Fancy Pants went down like a vulture-shaped bowling pin. The two animals scrambled to get to their feet, but I scooped up my cat.

Half an hour earlier, this cat had been left to freeze to death. Now she was in the ultimate hunting ground. I wondered what went through her mind as I popped her into the cage and closed it.

I spent the next ten minutes luring the vulture back into his enclosure. He was convinced that every other bird had Girl Scout Cookies and eyed them with what he probably thought was a threatening look, but it really came off as goofy.

At long last, I herded him back into the enclosure, where he ran over to Philby, locked in her cage, looking just as angry as she had when I'd found her outside.

The bird walked all the way around the cage, looking the cat up and down. Philby met his gaze with furious intensity. Finally, the vulture climbed on top of the cage, made some weird noises, and barfed through the bars onto the cat.

*   *   *

"It's your own fault," I said for the fiftieth time.

I'd managed to finagle the feline into the sink of the restroom and was rinsing her off. By the way, regurgitated Oreos are a pain to get out of white fur. Philby gave me the stink eye even as I tried to blot her dry with the brown paper towels from the motion-sensitive dispenser.

Why hadn't I packed any towels in my go bag? I'd have to do that next time. The paper towels didn't work out very well, and I had one angry cat when I was done.

"Now we have to go." I sighed. The safe house wasn't turning out to be very safe after all.

My cat yowled as I stuffed her back into my coat, collected my things, and left after making sure things were marginally clean. Someone was going to find some seriously agitated birds and several pounds of wet cat hair and paper towels in the bathroom. I kind of wished I could be there to see that.

Back in Rex's car, I realized I couldn't exactly go on the run with Philby. If anything, she'd proven to be a loose cannon in the aviary. Not that I thought Rex was being held in a place surrounded by bird guards (in which case, I would need her). It was too cold to leave her in the car.

Bart! Philby had to have been taken from Rex's house! Was Bart okay? I called the house but got no answer.

So I drove to Kelly's house.

"What's going on?" Kelly yawned as she opened the door. She stared at the large bulge in my coat. "What is that?"

Philby popped her head out of my chest, and Kelly hurried us inside, where I told her about the clue while not telling her about the zoo.

"I can't keep her here," she said. "Robert's allergic."

I nodded. "I know. I just want you to take her to Rex's house and give her to Bart."

I thought about this. Either Bart was going crazy, looking for the missing cat, or he didn't even realize she was gone. The third option would be that whoever took her, tied him up...or worse.

"You should probably make sure he's okay too," I added.

I waited for her to argue, but instead, Kelly took the damp cat from me. "What are you going to do now?"

"I'm going to Linda's. We have all four clues now, and that means Rex has run out of time."

"It's two o'clock in the morning!" Kelly said.

"That's a good point. Call her and let her know I'm on my way so I don't surprise her." With that, I left.

Was I too cavalier with my co-leader? Not really. She'd drugged me three times. Paybacks were hell.

Linda met me at the door, fully dressed. I smiled. She was a real trouper. And she had cinnamon rolls and hot tea waiting. Forget trouper! She was the best!

The teacher looked over the last clue. "And you said that there wasn't anything else? There should be something. This gives you no insight into the endgame."

I had to agree. The kidnapper left us hanging with this one. I took a sheet of paper and wrote out the four clues, trying to see if there was something we'd missed.

*Wedding traditions as good as gold...Let's start out with Something Old.*

*Weddings make a family of two...Let's add in Something New.*

*There will be no honeymoon tomorrow...Let's turn next to Something Borrowed.*

*This is the bride's very last clue...Let us end with Something Blue.*

"I don't suppose there's an anagram in there somewhere?" I asked hopefully.

Linda shook her head. "I don't think so.

"Does it look to you like there's something hidden in these clues?"

Linda studied them while I wolfed down three cinnamon rolls. She took out a pencil and played with the words, rearranging them into several combinations. But all she came up with was nonsense.

"Are you wet?" my former teacher asked. "In this weather?"

I nodded. "Wet cat. You don't want to know."

"I'll grab a sweatshirt. You get that coat off and the shirt too."

Something scratched me as I unzipped the coat and fell on the floor when I removed it. It was just Philby's collar. Must've come off when he was under my coat. I picked it up and set it on the table. Linda returned with a sweatshirt, and I went into the bathroom to change.

"Much better," I said as I joined her.

She was staring at the collar.

"That's just my cat's collar. It came off in my shirt."

And then I froze. Philby didn't wear a collar. I'd tried several times to put one on her, but she always managed to shrug it off. This was easy because her body was larger than her neck and head.

"Did you notice?" Linda handed it to me. "It's blue."

"And it has one of my old Girl Scout Leader pins on it," I murmured.

Linda said, "Something old. And the collar is brand new."

I almost dropped it. "And it's something blue!"

We scrutinized the collar and found that the loop that held it all together was a ring. A gold wedding ring.

"Something borrowed!" Linda said.

But I didn't hear her. Pulling it off the collar, I looked for the inscription that I hoped wasn't there.

*To R from M with love.*

It was Rex's wedding ring.

# CHAPTER SEVENTEEN

It felt like the air had been sucked out of my lungs. I squeezed the ring in the palm of my hand as if that would bring him back. We were out of time. We'd failed. I had no idea where to look for my missing fiancé. I'd blown it. Rex was still in danger, if he wasn't already dead.

"Merry!" Linda tugged on my elbow, and I turned to stare at her. "Look!" She held up the collar, showing me the underside. A piece of paper had been folded and taped there.

"There's always hope." She patted me on the shoulder and then worked on removing the piece of paper.

Linda Willard unfolded it and laid it on the table.

"It's sudoku!" she cried. "I can solve this!"

"But there's nothing highlighted." I shook my head. "All we'll have is a bunch of numbers. How will that help?"

"Merry Wrath!" The teacher drew herself up to her full height, which was still a foot shorter than mine. "What have I taught you about giving up before trying something?"

I slouched, chastened. "You don't give up until you've tried and exhausted all options."

"That's right. I'll get to work." She sat at the table and began.

I walked into the living room and checked the windows. No police. Maybe they'd given up on the idea that I was the bad guy. Ted Weir wasn't so bad. This was his job. He'd make a fine detective someday. I shouldn't be so hard on him. And he had Kevin Dooley for a partner. The man deserved a prize for that.

Sheriff Carnack was another matter. While we weren't close, he had helped me with a couple of cases. He knew about my past, and I was sure he trusted me. But back at the police station, he didn't say a word. And it made me worry. But Carnack had given me carte blanche to investigate.

My cell buzzed. It was Kelly.

"Is Bart okay?" I asked before she could speak.

"He's fine. He'd been sleeping and woke up to find the back door open and Leonard barking. I dropped off Philby."

I breathed a sigh of relief. "Thank you. Go back to bed. I'll call you in a few hours."

Next I dialed Riley. He answered on the first ring.

"Merry! Where are you?"

Awww. He sounded concerned.

"At Linda's. She's working on the last clue."

"I'll be right over," he said and hung up.

I watched at the window. His neighborhood wasn't far from here. After what I'd gone through this night, I should have been exhausted. Instead, I was hopped up like a speed junkie who'd been given an adrenaline shot. We were close.

"I found something," he said as I answered the door.

Back in the living room, we sat down. He pulled a piece of paper out of his pocket. I was getting kind of sick of paper clues.

"Lana," Riley said, "might be here after all. She's gotten in touch with an old ally—Vladimir Shoshenko. He's in Omaha."

I snatched the piece of paper. "Phone records?"

He pointed at several highlighted numbers. "The Feds are watching him. Have been for months. On a gun-running charge. According to this guy I worked with there, they kept hearing phone calls between him and a woman he called Svetlana."

I felt like I already knew this. Sort of. I asked a different question.

"Riley, your theory that Rex and I have crossed paths. Have you thought about that?"

He frowned. "Not really. I kind of gave up on it. Why?"

This was going to sound crazy, but Riley was used to that with me. "Because I have the feeling that something like that did happen. Only it was something Rex did before I did." I explained the dreams.

"Okay," he reasoned. "You think that Rex, in his past, came across something that you later were involved in? Interesting."

I threw my hands up. "But the possibilities are endless. And I have no idea what it could be!"

Riley looked at the kitchen. "We have to start somewhere. Let's go through your tenure at the Agency."

I was desperate for anything that would help. And it was the one thing Riley and I could recall together. For the next two hours, we ran through our field assignments. I can't tell you about them because many of them are still classified. Except for the time we got "married" in Norway.

"Maybe that's it?" I asked. "You kind of married me, and Rex is going to marry me?"

He sat back. "You might be onto something there. Has Rex ever been to Norway?"

I shrugged. "I don't know. I haven't discussed it with him."

It was hard to be a spy, even an ex-spy, and know that there were some things you just couldn't discuss with your loved ones. Now, I regretted that because there was possibly something in my past that connected with Rex.

"I think we've hit a dead end," I said finally. "It was a good theory. What made you come up with it?"

Riley stared off into space. "I don't know. It just popped into my head. When Bobby Ray Pratt's body was put in my house, I couldn't figure out how I fit into this being revenge on you and Rex."

"Well, like I said, it was a good idea. Those dreams were probably just psychosomatic."

He smiled. "You know, I took a class in that in college. It was pretty interesting. The things you say can pop up in your dreams. Sometimes they really do mean something."

"And sometimes they don't?" I added.

"And sometimes they don't. Anyway, it was just a low-level class that I needed for my transfer."

I smothered a yawn. "I thought you went to Cal State all four years. You majored in political science, right?"

"True. But I started somewhere else and transferred. I missed the ocean. But hey, sounds like you know more about me than you do your fiancé," he teased.

I shook my head. "That's not true. I know that he also majored in political science. At Iowa State."

Riley's jaw dropped.

"What is it?" I suddenly felt very alert.

"The school I transferred from"—he took a deep breath—"was Iowa State."

It was as if the sound was turned way down and the lights were turned way up.

I could barely get the words out. "What years were you there?"

"2006 to 2008, I think."

"Rex was there 2006 to 2010." My voice was barely a whisper. "It's you! *You* are our connection."

We sat there in silence, our minds working through the problem. This was a puzzle on another level. While Linda was in the kitchen scratching out the answers to her sudoku, we were concentrating on ours.

"You must've had a class together," I mused. "Or dated the same girl?"

That would be something, because Riley was a player. He dated more women in his lifetime than a normal man after three reincarnations as George Clooney. The good news was that Rex only dated a few women. I'd heard their names and even met one, but was that the connection?

"Well, we do have similar tastes in women." He grinned.

"You and I dated for, like, a minute. Focus!"

He shook his head. "I don't think it was a girl. Rex is more serious about relationships than I am. I dated a lot of, shall we say, less serious girls in college."

I sighed. "What does it mean anyway? Maybe nothing. Coincidences happen all the time."

He held up one finger. "It might explain how I became involved. If this is about you and Rex, why leave the body at my house?"

"Because you and the victim worked at the CIA? Because you're related to Vy Todd?"

"Both good points," he agreed.

"Besides," I grumbled. "This might be only about one of us. They might be throwing stuff about the unrelated party just to get us on the wrong track."

"Or go in circles…" Riley said.

We were spinning our wheels. And getting nowhere fast. Our only hope was in a bunch of numbers.

I picked up my cell and punched the keypad.

"Who are you calling at this hour?" Riley asked.

"Officer Weir," I said through the ringing. "I need his help, and I think it's time I turned myself in."

Ted met us at the station. Linda assured us that she'd keep working the puzzle but thought it would take a while.

The young policeman rubbed his eyes. He looked like he'd just gotten out of bed.

"I'm sorry about running," I said quickly. "I just thought…"

He held his hands up. "It's okay. We think the evidence that casts suspicion on you is worthless. Sorry about that. We have to follow every lead…"

I finished, "…and you were just doing your job. I get it."

Even though he'd accused me, this young man had potential. I was sure that with Rex's guidance, he'd become an excellent detective and a credit to the force.

"Can we start again?" he asked earnestly.

I shook my head. "Let's just move on like it never happened."

Daylight broke through the windows. I'd been up all night. My body was feeling the pains from the car accident. At least I'd eaten. Still, we went over all of the clues so far. I just left out the part about the zoo. No one needed to know about that.

"I can bring you up to speed too," Ted said. "We got a wiretap for Vy Todd. And she's been talking about some mystery thing that's going to make her crew, aka Oak and Winters, very happy."

I rubbed my eyes. "You did? Did she say anything about where they're keeping Rex?"

"Not yet. But Des Moines is on it, and they've promised to keep me updated if it applies to our case."

"Do you think it might not?" That would bring Lana's and Riley's and Rex's connection theories back into play.

Ted's eyes shone with empathy. "I'm not sure, but I have a good feeling about this. Remember, it was Vy Todd's fingerprints at your house." He pointed at Riley. "And we have a witness who remembers seeing her at Marlowe's grocery store the day of your wedding."

I perked up. "So she was in town the day Spitz was murdered—that puts her near the scene of the crime." Could it really be this easy? I hoped so.

"Is she connected to any buildings in the area?" Riley asked. "Any place where she could keep a hostage?"

Ted scratched his head. "Let me ask. Hold on." He stepped away from his desk and called somebody. It could be the Des Moines police department or the state police. I didn't care as long as there were results.

"This could be it!" Riley said. "We might find Rex today!"

I would've been jumping for joy, but suddenly, with the case almost over, I was crashing. Hard. Riley noticed. He knew from experience that I did not do overnights well. He ran from the room and returned with an energy drink. I gulped it.

"The whole thing about the connection was a red herring, I guess," I said when done.

He nodded. "I guess so. But it kept us busy. That's good."

I could feel my energy level growing a little. When this was over, I was going to pass out for a few days. I hoped no one would mind. But I wanted to get married right away, once we got Rex back. Would the pastor mind marrying Rex to an unconscious woman in a three-thousand-dollar dress?

I wondered, "Do you think we might find Rex before Linda finishes the puzzle?"

"We might." Riley shrugged. "But don't call her off of it just yet."

"Great news!" Ted beamed as he joined us. "It just so happens that Vy Todd's cousin rents a little shop here in town."

"Really?" I jumped up and hugged him. "Where?"

He laughed. "You're not going to believe it."

Five minutes later we were standing outside of a florist shop. My florist shop. The one where Lewis Spitz had worked.

"She's connected to this shop?" I asked. "Well, that explains why my flowers were ridiculously expensive…"

"The cousin rented the place when Vy was still in prison, so she worked through a proxy." Ted looked around.

The officer pulled his gun from his holster. That was when I noticed that Riley had a gun too. My bag was still in Rex's car at Linda's.

"Give me your gun," I said to Riley.

He gave me a look. "No. Just get behind me."

I gave him a look that beat out his look. "Give. Me. The. Gun. I'm going in first."

"Are you serious? You've been in a car accident, been doped, and haven't slept in at least twenty-four hours."

I turned my full glare on him. "I'm the bride. That's my groom in there. The first person he's going to see is me. And the first person who's going to shoot Vy Todd is me!"

Riley looked at Ted. Ted looked at Riley. Riley handed me his gun.

I tried the door. Locked. I motioned for Riley and Ted to sweep around each side of the building. Riley took the right. Ted disappeared on the left. The idea was to cover all bases and look for other exits. Then they'd come and join me. I didn't wait for them as I kicked in the door.

I'd sent them off to get them out of the way. Kicking in the door was basically breaking and entering, but so was using lockpicks. This method was faster. Ted might've stopped me from barreling in like that, so I sent him away. I only had seconds though. They'd have heard the crash and would be joining me soon.

The building was dark, probably because it was early in the morning. I slipped in, gun blazing. I wasn't taking any chances, but I wasn't going to let them get to Rex before I did.

"What are you doing?" Riley hissed in my ear. They found me sooner than I'd thought.

"We have to do things by the book," Ted whispered.

I ignored both of them and swept the small shop from right to left. The door behind the counter caught my attention, and I hurdled the counter and opened it. A basement. Perfect. Riley and Ted chose not to jump over the counter, but it didn't look as cool. To tell you the truth, I was surprised I'd made it over.

"I haven't heard anything," Ted said. "There's no one here."

"Great," I said grimly.

His arm came out in front of me. "I'm going first, Ms. Wrath. This is my job. And it's nonnegotiable. I can't allow a civilian to take the risk."

I opened my mouth to argue, but Riley cut me off. "He's right. Let him do his job."

I couldn't fight both of them, so I stepped aside and allowed the officer to pass me. In my rational mind, I knew he was right. Besides, he was wearing body armor.

Riley got between us, which I didn't like. He had a flashlight, and he aimed it into the darkness below. The stairs were wooden and rickety. The basement floor was cement. The rest was dark with a strong odor of mildew.

We descended carefully, Riley illuminating Ted's steps. The rookie's form was very good. This case was certainly a trial by fire for him. Being last, I made sure to look behind me every now and then. At long last, we touched the floor and fanned out.

We were in a large cement room with shelves covered with boxes of floral things. If we had time, I'd check those boxes. But Rex could be a few feet away, and that was my priority. My heart skipped a beat in anticipation.

The first thing I'd do was crush him in an embrace. Then I'd go on a killing spree, taking down everyone who had him. I probably wouldn't tell Ted or Rex about that part though.

Ahead of us was a long, dark hallway. Which meant rooms on either side. And one of those rooms might have my fiancé in it. I surged ahead, only to have Riley grab my arm and pull me back.

"What are you doing?" I whispered furiously.

"You're leading with emotions, not reason," he explained. "What's the first thing we need to do?"

I sighed. "Check for booby traps."

He was right. Charging into the unknown was dangerous, and I wanted to be at my own wedding, whenever that would be.

Riley crouched down, skimming his flashlight along the surface of the floor. I glanced at the top of the stairs as my former handler examined every inch of the doorway to the hall. It was a good thing he was thorough because the light glinted off a piece of piano wire strung across the doorframe.

He followed the wire, which was connected to a loaded crossbow. I'd be a shish kebab right now if he hadn't pulled me back. I took a couple of deep breaths, trying to steady my thoughts as Riley disarmed the crossbow and cut the wire with a pocketknife. He stood up and nodded to Ted and me.

Ted went first again, with Riley shining the flashlight over the officer's shoulder and me bringing up the rear. There were two rooms total, one on each side. After a quick scan for traps, Ted reached out and turned the knob. The two men ran into the room, sweeping his gun from left to right, while I stayed in the corridor and covered them.

Ted reappeared with Riley behind him, shaking his head. No Rex there. We repeated the procedure with the next room with the same result. I was disappointed. I thought for sure Rex was in this basement.

"Aaaaaaaargh!" A man came screaming at us from the end of the hall, holding a large knife.

It was Harvey Oak. He was closing in on us when Ted fired two shots, center mass. The man dropped like a stone. Riley disarmed him and felt for a pulse. He turned to us and shook his head. Harvey Oak was dead.

Ted was stunned into what looked like a state of shock. Riley gently took the rookie's gun and led him back up the stairs, clearing the way. I again brought up the rear.

"No Rex." I sighed once we were at the top of the stairs.

Riley shook his head. "Sorry, Merry. I'd hoped he was there too."

Ted was walking around looking at things but seemed to be in a daze.

"Are you alright?" I asked.

He shook his head. "I've never shot anyone before…let alone killed anyone."

Riley brought him a chair, and the kid sat.

"If it helps," I said, placing a hand on his shoulder, "it gets easier."

Yes, that was a morbid thing to say. But when I shot someone for the first time, my first handler, Frank, had said that to me, and it'd helped. Frank was a good guy, but after the Marco incident in Turkey, he'd retired early and as far as I knew was still drinking his way around the DC Metro area.

That was one good thing about Riley—he had no qualms about the job. And someday Ted Weir would be okay with it too. He just needed a little time.

I called Dr. Body and the station. Kevin Dooley arrived with a box of half-eaten donuts. To my complete shock, he offered Ted one.

"Go ahead." I nodded. "The sugar helps."

The rookie chewed slowly. Color had started to return to his face by the time the coroner arrived. I walked her through the scene as Riley gave Officer Dooley a statement. We both made it look like Ted was the hero, which he was.

Soo Jin knelt beside the body and ran her hands over it. "Looks like two shots to the heart did him in. I'll take him back to the morgue to make sure, but it's pretty cut and dry."

By the time I got back upstairs, Officer Weir seemed a bit more normal. He was talking to the forensics team and giving them orders. Riley and I went outside.

"So, Harvey Oak is involved," I said.

Riley agreed. "Looks that way. One down, two more to go."

"Do you think she kept Rex here at one time?"

He shook his head. "The rooms were full of boxes. There's no room for a person."

My shoulders slumped. "Then this was a bust."

He looked back at the shop. "Not necessarily. We know that Vy and Oak were up to something. And Ted shot his first criminal."

"I don't think he's too happy about that."

We waited on the sidewalk until the forensic team and Dr. Body left. Officers Weir and Dooley locked up the building. Ted called the Des Moines police, asking them to pick Vy Todd up.

"I'm taking you home," Riley said. "You're totally beat."

"But Linda…Rex…" I protested weakly.

He was right. I was wiped out. The last of my adrenaline gave out in the basement, and I was running on fumes. I fell asleep in Riley's SUV before we even pulled out of the lot.

\* \* \*

I awoke in a strange room. I'd been so tired I hadn't even dreamt. Darkness filled the curtains of a bedroom that was decorated in neutral tones. An overstuffed chintz chair sat by the window, next to a small table with a dimly lit lamp.

This wasn't my house. Riley said he was taking me home. Oh. Maybe he meant his home. This must be his guest room. It was very tasteful. The kind of room you could sleep comfortably in.

I'd wanted to be in my house, just in case something came up. But I couldn't be angry with Riley. My guess was he wanted to watch over me and knew I'd be safe here. That was nice. Annoying, but nice.

I got out of bed and realized I was wearing men's pajamas. I was still wearing my bra and panties, or Riley would be getting a black eye for his trouble. I opened the door and walked into the kitchen.

The room was cheery and brightly lit. Riley was wearing an actual apron, standing at the stove, stirring something that smelled like it came from heaven.

"What's that?" I said.

He turned and grinned. "I like you in my pajamas."

"Don't start," I warned. "I'd punch you for changing me, except that I'm still kind of tired."

I sat at a small table. "What are you making?"

"Stew." He ladled some into a bowl and set it before me.

I inhaled the scent of beef, carrots, and potatoes. Riley set a freshly warmed baguette and butter dish next to me, and I dug in. It was magical. Maybe it was because I was hungry. Maybe it was the best stew in the world. It didn't matter, because I ate two bowls and half the baguette.

"Want some more?" Riley grinned. He'd had only one bowl and a salad. Ridiculous!

"No." I waved him off. "That was amazing. And I needed that."

"Good. Glad to help." He carried the dishes to the sink and began washing up.

Through the kitchen window I noticed it was dark. "What time is it?"

"Seven. You didn't sleep too long."

"Where's my cell?" I started to panic when I realized I didn't have it.

He handed it to me. That was the second time in a couple of days where he'd confiscated my phone. Between that and Kelly's drugging spree, I felt more like an invalid teenager than a grown-up woman.

"Any news?" I asked as I turned on the phone. No messages.

Riley shook his head. "Sorry."

I fiddled with a loose thread on my sleeve and asked a question I wasn't sure I wanted to know the answer to.

"It's been nine days. What if Rex is…is…" I couldn't finish. "It's just been so long. I'm not feeling very hopeful."

Riley poured me a glass of wine. "Here. Drink this."

I did.

"You want to know what I think? I think Rex is still alive. The kidnapper is keeping him alive because they want you to solve the puzzle. I think it's going to come to a showdown."

I took another drink. "One that I'm going to win." Something else bothered me, but less so. "What about Juliette Dowd?"

He frowned. "Either she's the villain or victim. I don't know which."

"We don't know anything about this whole mess," I grumbled, polishing off the wine.

"Do you have any idea why she was in Rex's house?"

I thought for a second or two. "She said she was looking for proof that I took him or killed him."

"Do you believe her?"

I thought about it. Juliette had been infatuated with Rex for most of her life. She didn't have it in her to kill him. Kidnap him maybe, but kill him?

"Yes. I don't want to. Frankly, I'd love to see her go to jail for kidnapping and murder. But I don't think she's involved."

Wow. I really did think that. Huh.

"What about Lana?" I pressed.

He sat down across from me. "I don't think she's part of this. We'd have seen her by now."

"I did see her," I insisted.

"But that's the only thing we have on her," Riley said. "And I'm still not convinced it's her."

"So it's Vy Todd and her gang... Why involve me? Why kill Bobby Ray, and how would she know about him?"

"Red herring?" he suggested.

It was kind of like when you were almost done with a puzzle. Only the last piece didn't fit. You crammed it in and considered cutting it to size, but in the end, you were left with a piece that didn't belong in that puzzle.

My cell buzzed. "Hey, Bart. Everything good?"

"Yeah," he monotoned. "We're low on food."

"I'll take care of it." I hung up and called Kelly, begging her to pick up and deliver some food to Betty's brother.

"Why do I have to do it?" she asked.

"Because you've drugged me three times, and I'm sure that breaks some sort of ethics thingy."

Her voice was measured. "Are you threatening me?"

"Yes." I hung up. She'd do it.

My cell buzzed again. I answered without looking. "Yes, Bart?"

"It's Linda. You'd better come over." She hung up.

＊　＊　＊

Riley didn't like it, and he told me so about four times on the drive over there. "It sounds like a trap," he said. "She didn't say she'd solved the puzzle. Maybe the kidnapper is using her to lure you over."

"That's why I have this." I racked the slide on a .45 I'd *borrowed* from Riley's gun safe. He stared at the gun and opened his mouth to speak.

"It's your own fault! You're still using the same password you used the whole time we worked together."

Was Riley right? Did the kidnapper have Linda too? If so, I was going to kill her twice. Maybe even three times, for Philby.

Linda met us at the door and ushered us into her kitchen. In spite of the fact that she'd been working on this for twenty-four hours at least, she looked rested and fresh. I, on the other hand, had dark circles under my eyes and unruly wet hair from a quick shower. And I was wearing yesterday's clothes.

"I think I've got it," she said excitedly. "I took all the numbers from the corner boxes and compared them to their corresponding letters of the alphabet. Since sudoku uses only numbers one through nine and there are twenty-six letters in the alphabet, every number has more than one letter. For example, the number one stands for letters A, J, and S."

"But if each number stood for three letters, how did you know which one was which?" I asked.

Linda smiled. "There are only five vowels. Words need vowels. So I went for A instead of J or S. Once I filled in the vowels, deciding which corresponding consonant went with it was pretty easy!"

Riley and I exchanged glances. "You could be a code breaker for the CIA!" I gushed. "What made you think of using the letters in the corners? I'd go with the ones in the center."

Linda shrugged. "It just made sense to me to do that." She handed me her notes.

*Bells are ringing and children singing.*

*There's educating to be done, in the spot where you once had fun.*

*All is waiting there for you, come along if you dare, when you've solved this clue.*

"What do you think it means?" Riley asked.

"Bells ringing could refer to the wedding," I mumbled. "Children and fun may be related to Girl Scouts. We've had a lot of fun at camp, and I've taught the girls things there."

"I don't think the last sentence means anything more than *come and get it*," Linda said.

I nodded. "I agree. It's the first two sentences we have to work on."

"The time is up," Riley said. "They're not messing around anymore. I think you have one shot to get this right. You can only go to one place."

I felt that in my gut he was absolutely right. The clue could be talking about a number of places, from the church we were supposed to get married in to Girl Scout Camp, to…

"I got it!" I screamed. "I know where Rex is!"

"Should we call Ted?" Riley asked.

I shook my head. "I don't think he's ready for another shootout. This one is for you and me. And we're going to need more weapons."

"I should go too," Linda said.

"No," I said gently. "These are dangerous people. I don't want to drag you into this."

"I can help," she insisted.

"Not this time." I hugged her. "But you've been amazing. I couldn't have done it without you."

Linda smiled. I loved having her help. But she couldn't get mixed up in a shootout.

Riley and I cleaned out his weapons cache. By the time we hit the road, it was late at night. We had two shotguns, two handguns, and four knives between us. My bloodlust was roaring. I was ready to get my fiancé and wreak some havoc on these people.

"You didn't tell me," Riley said as he slapped the magazine into a 9mm and racked the slide, "where are we going?"

I smiled. "Back to the beginning. And I think I know who the villain is."

# CHAPTER EIGHTEEN

———

"This place?" Riley asked as I pulled into the old elementary school.

The building was condemned, but for some reason the city still hadn't demolished it. And it was the scene of a major shootout a few years back. One that involved me.

"You think it's Lana," Riley said.

I nodded. "I think it's Lana."

We got out of the car and walked up to the front door. The knob came off in my hand. On the way over, we'd toyed with going stealth on this...parking a few blocks away, sneaking in through a window.

But I was sick and tired of messing around. This time, I was going to confront things once and for all. Riley and I were taking this psycho out, permanently. Let her know we were coming. She wasn't going to kill us until we found Rex. There was no point in hiding.

It was dark inside. With his flashlight, Riley lit up the corridors with the sagging and rusting lockers.

"The gym?" he asked.

"We'll check there first," I agreed.

The school was laid out in a square. One hallway wrapped around the gym. A simple layout. There were two doorways into the gym, and Riley took the one on the left, while I took the one on the right. We'd agreed that he'd wait a few minutes after I'd entered before he made his appearance. It was a small thing, but it might catch Lana off guard, if even for a second.

The gym was brightly lit. There was no sign of Juliette, Rex, or their captor, but the lights meant we were in the right place. *Bells ringing* meant school bells. *Children singing* pointed to the elementary school, as did *educating*. And while I did have fun here as a kid, I knew she was talking about a very different kind of fun a couple of years back.

"Lana!" I shouted. "Lana!"

A voice close behind me said, "Why are you shouting?"

I jumped and spun in the air to find a confused police officer behind me. Ted was looking around, sweeping the room with his gun.

"What are you doing here?" I hissed.

"I followed you," he said, red color creeping up his neck. "I told you not to do this stuff alone!"

Damn. And I was going to murder Lana in cold blood. Now I'd have to wait for her to come at me first so it would look like self-defense. Not only that, Ted was in way over his head here, and I didn't want the rookie getting hurt.

"You shouldn't be here," I said as menacingly as possible while my mind raced for a reason why. "I'm not even sure that this is the right place." I didn't mention my concern that he'd just shot someone for the first time and might not be able to pull the trigger.

He didn't buy it. "I can't let a couple of civilians get hurt on my watch."

Riley walked in on the other side, stopping in his tracks when he spotted the policeman. That was when the curtains went up on the stage. Spotlights shone down on a body in a burlap bag as it strained against the ropes and chair it was tied to.

Instead of coming to me, Riley ran for the stage and landed in a single leap next to the chair. His hands worked furiously, and I ran to the stage, hopped on (with considerably less grace), and checked the wings. There was one door in the back that led down into the basement.

"It's Juliette, isn't it?" I said as I joined Riley on stage.

He removed the last rope and the bag fell. An angry redhead with duct tape on her mouth scowled at us, squeaking what I can only assume to be cuss words.

"How did you know?" Riley asked as he pulled the tape free.

"The body size. She's too small to be Rex. Which means we aren't done here yet." I kept my gun up and watched the gym. Ted was gone.

Officer Weir shouted from the hallway. "I see him! This way!"

Oh no! He'd run off half-cocked. This kid was going to get himself killed unless I caught up.

I looked at Riley. "Stay here with her."

He shook his head. "No. I'm coming with you."

Juliette shrieked a high-pitched flow of words I couldn't understand. I got in her face and held her shoulders.

"You stay here," I commanded. "It's not safe."

The woman looked from me to Riley and nodded. She was angry but scared enough to listen.

I ran into the hall to see Ted's back disappearing through another door that led to the basement.

"That idiot is going to get shot," I mumbled under my breath.

"He just wants to help," Riley said.

We started running, but I drew up short at the door. "Take the door on the stage," I whispered. "It goes to the basement too, but you'll come out in the middle."

Riley nodded, and I steeled myself before running into the rabbit hole. Halfway down the stairs I could hear Ted running and shouting, "Stop! In the name of the law!"

Yeesh. I was almost embarrassed for him. We'd have to work on his lingo. I hit the bottom stair. I knew where I was going. The basement was divided into food storage—which no longer existed since the building had been abandoned—boxes of old memorabilia, and one room that was used for theatrical purposes.

I knew this because I was in exactly one play in school. It was *The Wizard of Oz*, and I'd been a tree. If Rex was here, that was where he was. I knew it.

A door slammed ahead, and I heard Ted scream. Damn! I ran to the door, but it was locked. Rearing back, I threw all of my weight against the area where the doorknob was. The rotting door splintered easily.

In the middle of the room, tied to a chair and slumped over with a bag over his head, was my fiancé, the love of my life, Detective Rex Ferguson. I didn't run to him, because this was a trap. In my head I warned him not to move.

Where was Ted Weir?

"You solved the last clue!" He sprang from behind the door, gun trained on me.

I leveled my gun at his head. "You?" I shrieked. "You're the bad guy?"

Ted gave me an ugly smile. "You didn't see that coming, did you?"

I shook my head. I really didn't. "Not Lana?" I asked. I could've kicked myself.

He frowned. "You didn't know it was me? I thought for sure you'd figure it out."

"How could I have known it was you?"

"I guess we really are that good." Ted grinned. "Right, Dad?"

Dad?

Prescott Winters III stepped out from behind a wardrobe. Dang it! I should've checked the wardrobe. He had a shotgun aimed a few inches from Rex's head.

"Drop the gun, please, Ms. Wrath," the murderer said.

I didn't mind a gun aimed at me, but a shotgun aimed at Rex was too much to bear. I did as I was told and turned to Ted. "You're working with the man who killed your mother?"

"Not my mother," Ted said. "My mother was Dad's first wife. A lovely Turkish lady named Reza."

"Turkish?" Something popped into my head. The first clue! The very first crossword listed Marco, the man who died under my watch years ago. It wasn't Lana at all. The fact that the kidnapper knew about that made me think it was another spy. "You knew Marco?"

Prescott nodded. "My brother-in-law. My first wife's baby brother. When he died, Reza couldn't live with it. She killed herself."

Ted snapped. "And it's your fault!"

I needed to stall until Riley found us. It was kind of amazing that Ted had forgotten about him.

I spoke up quickly and a little louder than usual. "How did you even find out about that? That mission is still classified!"

Ted turned and shut what was left of the door. I thought about rushing him, but Prescott winked at me and pushed the gun closer to Rex's head. *Riley! Where are you?*

"I had a few drinks with your old pal, Frank," Ted said. "The guilt of my uncle's death nearly killed him."

Prescott piped up, "Actually, it did kill him."

"Oh, right." Ted nodded. "It killed him."

My jaw dropped, and my heart twisted. "Frank's dead?"

"Alcohol poisoning. A nasty way to go," Prescott answered with a huge smile. "And now that I have you two here, in the same room, we can wrap up everything and avenge our family."

"You are the mastermind," I said to Prescott.

"Hey!" Ted whined. "I helped! He couldn't have done it without me!"

His father rolled his eyes, but I didn't think Ted saw that. "Of course, son." He gave me a wink. "It really was my idea. I spent a long time in prison, which gave me all the time I needed to come up with revenge. When I found out my boy here was perfectly positioned to carry out my plans, well, it was a no-brainer."

Ted frowned. Something about what his dad said upset him. Was it because Prescott implied he'd used Ted for his own gain?

Where was Riley? I could really use him right now. I looked at the door and drew Ted's attention.

He squinted at me. "Are you looking for your other handler? I'm afraid he's probably dead. I set a trap on the other staircase in case you two split up. I knew *you'd* follow me. I just didn't know for sure if he would."

"What kind of trap?" I folded my arms over my chest. "Don't you remember Riley in the flower shop? He watched for that trap. He's found and disarmed this one too."

The room shook with a nearby explosion.

Prescott's eyebrows went up. "You were saying?"

No! Riley couldn't be dead. He was too smart for that. Wasn't he?

"I've been working with Dad on this plan for so long. I couldn't possibly have left anything to chance. In fact, once I finish you two off here, I'm heading over to see your old teacher, Linda Willard."

My mouth dropped open. "What? Why? She doesn't know anything! I didn't even tell her where we were going!"

Weir stopped and stared at me like I was an idiot. "Because I can." He rolled his eyes. "She knows enough, so she has to die, and you need to know this."

There was a flash of something outside the splintered door.

I threw my hands into the air. "I have to admit, you had me fooled."

"And the CIA. After Frank told me about my uncle's untimely murder, he named you. The only problem was, I was looking for Finn Czrygy. Not Merry Wrath. Bravo, by the way." Ted's smile was genuine. Genuine psychopath. Prescott had taken full advantage of it. And I'd missed it.

"Thanks," I grumbled, my mind racing to put together a plan that I wasn't sure I'd live to carry out.

"Very proud of you, my boy," Prescott said. "But I think we can leave the teacher out of this. Remember what I said about overkill?"

Ted stomped his feet and turned red. "I want her dead!" he sputtered. "I want all of them dead!"

Oh yeah. Prescott was definitely the mastermind. And Ted's behavior was a ray of hope. I could work with a meltdown. There was that movement behind the door again. Was it Riley? A vagrant? A very large rat?

"Son," Prescott said firmly, "we still have other schemes in motion. Killing too many people would increase the risk. I warned you about that."

My eyebrows went up, and I looked to Ted.

"Dad didn't want me to kill that florist or your replacement at the CIA." Ted shot his dad a sullen glance. "Said it was too much. That we shouldn't kill anyone but you and Rex once we got you in here."

Ah. So that was the plan. Reunite the couple and kill them.

"Why drag it out?" I asked. "Why have me run all over town for nine days? Why keep Rex alive?"

Ted rolled his eyes. "Duh! Because it tormented you! Dad wanted to finish you both off quickly, but I was enjoying it too much." He glared at his father. "It's what a real villain would do!"

Yeah…a Bond villain. Not anyone in real life. But I wasn't about to tell him that. Ted was right—these last several days were torture. And looking at the shape Rex was in, I'd say it was that way for both of us.

"It's called *creative license*." He beamed. "And I nailed it."

Prescott sighed like a parent with a naughty toddler. "I know you think so, son. But now we've got two murders on our hands. In a moment, it'll be four. You need to learn—less is better. You can't get greedy in these situations. It's tacky."

Ted narrowed his eyes. "Don't call me *son*! You were never there for me! You left me in foster care way longer than you should have!"

Whoa. He snapped quickly. While I was entertained by this family tiff, I needed to exploit it. I held up my hands and walked slowly backward, toward Rex. The two men didn't even notice.

"I told you," the older man said evenly, "I married Jeannie for her money. I wasn't *abandoning* you to foster care." His words were nice and all, but the way he said "abandoning" sounded a bit sarcastic. He really did use his son.

This relationship was seriously messed up. Awesome! I stepped back once more and felt Rex's knee connect with the back of my leg. Prescott's shotgun was wavering as he tried to calm down his lunatic son. Ted was waving his arms, and his gun all over the place.

"Foster care was awful!" Ted screamed. "I was shifted around five times in one year! And all that time I was waiting for you to kill your wife, collect the inheritance, and get me!"

Prescott held up the hand that wasn't on the gun and spoke soothingly. "Which I did, remember?"

I was about four feet from the shotgun. Prescott's finger was still on the trigger, but the way he held it with one hand was just unsteady enough that I might have a chance. My chief concern was Rex. If I got the shotgun, Ted could regain his senses and shoot Rex. I couldn't risk that.

"Don't patronize me, boy," Prescott's voice was like iron. "This is my plan. You're lucky I let you participate."

Ted was purple with rage. "I should kill you too and be done with it, Dad!"

The door slowly opened, and a hand appeared near the floor, holding a homemade explosive device. The men didn't see Riley set it on the floor, but they could at any second. I lunged for the shotgun, surprising the older man, who just gave it up.

*Boom!*

An explosion went off just as Ted and I were drawing a bead on each other, but from what I could see, Ted was no more.

"Why didn't you use your gun?" I snapped at Riley as he trained his pistol on Prescott.

He shrugged. "I thought this was better."

"And the explosion we heard?" I started untying my fiancé, who was still unconscious.

"My shotgun," Riley said. "I always travel with one souped-up shell overloaded with powder."

Rex fell forward into my arms, and I pulled off the mask. He was dazed and maybe a bit dehydrated and starved. But he was okay.

"Merry?" His eyes fluttered open.

"Hi, honey!" I nearly crushed him in a hug. "You're a little late for our wedding, but you can make it up to me."

"Oh good," he said weakly. "How long have I been gone?"

"Nine days," I answered.

"Oh no!" He gasped. "The fee on my rented tux is going to be outrageous." Then he smiled at me, and I knew everything was going to be okay.

# CHAPTER NINETEEN

———

It wasn't a church, and there weren't three hundred guests, but four days later, Rex and I tied the knot with a justice of the peace at the courthouse, surrounded by Robert and Riley as groomsmen, Kelly and Soo Jin as bridesmaids, and ten little girls in the ugliest flower girl dresses imaginable.

I wore my very expensive wedding dress, and Kelly and Soo Jin wore their bridesmaids dresses. The only addition to the wedding party was Riley. Rex had been so grateful for his help that he made him a groomsman next to Kelly's husband, Robert. And it didn't even bother me.

"Hello, Mrs. Ferguson," Rex grinned and pulled me in for a lovely kiss.

I could've gotten lost in that kiss. My emotions had been overflowing since the minute I found him. Wrapping my arms tight around him, I returned that kiss, running my fingers through his hair.

"Ahem." Kelly cleared her throat.

Oh, right. The girls were here. This had to stay PG. I pulled back just in time to see Betty make gagging noises as Lauren shrieked something about not being able to unsee that, whatever that means.

I looked back at Rex and smiled. "Actually, I was going to talk to you about that. I'm thinking of keeping my name. Is that okay?"

Rex looked me in the eye. "It's absolutely okay. I don't really care what your name is as long as you're mine."

Which was the right thing to say, as my troop broke out in spontaneous applause. The little feminists apparently approved.

He grinned at them before turning back to me. "There's something else I need to say. And it will be the only time you'll ever hear these words from me."

I held my breath, wondering if I was about to get chastised for putting myself in danger to rescue him.

"Yes?" I asked uncertainly.

"Thank you"—he tipped my chin up with his thumb—"for interfering this time."

That earned him another kiss, and as our lips met, I noticed that there was a surprising lack of gagging.

\* \* \*

Ted Weir didn't die from his injuries, and after a short stay at the hospital under armed guard, he was well enough to get a trip to jail. It turned out that Harvey Oak had been working with Ted's father. To avoid that coming out when Oak attacked us at the flower shop, Ted had shot him dead. Combined with the murder of my florist, Lewis Spitz, and CIA agent Bobby Ray Pratt, and two counts of kidnapping, he was going away for a long time.

Prescott Winters III sang like a bird, selling his son out so he could make a deal for one of those posh white-collar crime prisons. He also volunteered additional information implicating Vy Todd in an opioid smuggling scheme. She went back to jail, and the governor refused to pardon her a second time.

Juliette Dowd was admitted to a mental hospital. The stress of being kidnapped didn't diminish her rage, so the authorities had her evaluated, by my counselor, Susan, no less. And she recommended a nice long stay at a lovely place in the country for an undetermined length of time. I should probably visit her. The girls made her a lovely card where she was an angry, sparkly unicorn.

I never did tell Rex about Ronni sending Juliette to his house to spy on me. When it comes to family, you just have to forgive and forget. With Juliette gone, the evil twin was out one conspirator, so I didn't expect any more shenanigans anytime soon.

Someday Ronni would like me. I wasn't quite sure how that would happen, but maybe if I brought her a dead animal as an olive branch, the evil twin might soften. But no matter what, I still wasn't eating the haggis she'd made. You have to draw the line somewhere.

Linda Willard enjoyed the thrill of the hunt so much that she decided to create crosswords and sudoku puzzles on her own. When the story of the retired teacher using her mad skills to help the police catch a murderer (cuz I'm still undercover, sort of) came out, she even got an offer from a major New York publisher, who gave her a nice advance for a book that will come out next summer.

Sheriff Carnack was so impressed that he had a little ceremony where he presented her with a Citizenship Award. I'd suggested a Medal for Murder, but for some reason, Rex nixed it. Linda accepted her award with grace as my troop applauded loudly and whistled from the audience.

In the meantime, my former teacher has offered to help out with my troop now and then. Kelly threw her arms around the woman when she offered. Yes, I know that sometimes I'm irresponsible, like having my girls play outside of a convicted smuggler's house. And Linda will make a wonderful addition to our troop. She's working on a special badge just for the troop, where they will learn how to solve puzzles. The girls are over the moon about it and requested a chapter on booby traps. I hope Linda doesn't come to regret Kelly's offer.

Bart house sat for us during our honeymoon. Turned out he was a real dog and cat whisperer. A very expensive whisperer, but the fact that Philby, Martini, and Leonard behaved so well around him was worth every penny.

As for Riley, he got his first case immediately after the explosion in the old school. A rich, young, gorgeous widow wanted him to find out if her late husband had been cheating on her. There seemed no merit to the case since the husband was dead and had left her a huge inheritance, but Riley accepted it anyway. I'd heard the two of them were on a little trip to Turks and Caicos for "work."

Rex and I managed to fly to our honeymoon island, a little later than we'd originally hoped. The sand and water were so soothing to the many bruises from my car accident. We found a peaceful, secluded beach on a small island in the middle of the ocean with no murders, kidnappings, or trouble of any kind. For a week we lay about in the sand, drinking silly cocktails that seemed to have been named in the 1950s by Rat Packers. And we found ways to distract ourselves from what happened. I'd tell you more, but it's classified. By me.

When we got back from our honeymoon, I decided to reward the girls for their help with a backstage tour of the aviary at the zoo. At first, the zoo refused, thinking that I'd broken in and washed a cat in the restroom for no apparent reason.

I denied it and wrote a large check, which changed their minds, and they agreed to the tour. Dr. Wulf, Obladi Zoo's director, offered to lead it personally. The girls adored Mr. Fancy Pants and missed him during the zoo's closing for the winter. Kelly brought Finn in a stroller, and I pretended I didn't know where anything was.

"This is really nice!" she whispered. "And how great is it that Linda wants to help out with the troop now and then?"

The retired teacher had whipped those girls into shape, to the point where they were politely lined up in an orderly fashion to take their turns giving Mr. Fancy Pants a cookie. The zoo was a little concerned about that at first, but another thousand-dollar check from me changed their minds. The trip was getting expensive…but totally worth it.

"I've been meaning to ask you," Kelly said, "how you got that wrong, thinking the woman in the video at the gas station was Lana?"

I hadn't gotten that wrong, but she didn't need to know that. "Near mental breakdown, I suppose."

Lana was out there, somewhere. I was sure of it. And even if she wasn't behind this, she was up to something. Riley still insisted I was mistaken, but I was going to keep my eyes open from here on out.

"And what about that mysterious phone call from Rex's cell?" she asked.

"Oh, right!" I'd forgotten to tell her. "Turns out Ted butt-dialed me on his way to the old school."

Kelly's jaw dropped. "He butt-dialed you? By accident?"

I rolled my eyes. "That's what it means. He had no idea it had happened. He only left the phone for me at the school so I'd know for sure he had Rex. He didn't mean to ever use the number."

It was just one of the many disclosures Sheriff Carnack got out of him before sending him to the slammer. I did ask if I could have ten minutes alone with the killer/kidnapper, but the sheriff wisely said *no*. Sadly, I had to put my pliers and car battery away.

"I love you, Mr. Fancy Pants!" Ava gasped as she handed him a Peanut Butter Patty.

The bird seemed to nod before gently taking the cookie from the little girl and crushing it in his beak.

"I love you too, Mr. Fancy Pants," Lauren gushed as she followed suit with another cookie.

The raptor repeated his gallant behavior. Funny…he'd never been that way with me. But it was good that he was acting so restrained around the kids.

"I'm so glad you stopped breaking in to see him," Kelly whispered, reminding me of a promise I'd made months ago and failed to keep (something else she didn't need to know). "I know you've missed him all of this time, but it was very adult of you."

"Oh yeah," I lied. "Like you said, it was a bad example to set for the girls, even if they never knew about it."

Kelly ignored the dig.

That was when the last girl, Betty, walked up and instead of one cookie, pulled a whole box from her bag and shook it in front of the bird. His eyes grew wide, and for a moment I thought he might attack. After all, Betty did violate our one-cookie policy with the zoo.

The zoo director deftly took the box from the girl and opened it. She then dumped it at the vulture's feet. Fancy Pants appeared to do a little bow before devouring the entire pile.

Dickie, the scarlet macaw, squawked loudly.

"Whoa." Kelly let out the breath she'd been holding. "I can't believe he was so calm! And since he hasn't had a visit from you since summer, you'd think he'd go crazy and tear the box to pieces!"

"Oh, absolutely," I said as I popped a pilfered cookie into my mouth.

She turned to look at me. "I'm really proud of you."

"For what?" I asked.

"Rescuing Rex, solving the case, your new friendship with Linda, and especially giving up your breaking and entering days."

I was about to thank her, but I didn't get the chance.

Dickie had had quite enough. He bobbed up and down on his perch before posing dramatically and shouting, "Philby!"

Kelly didn't talk to me for the rest of the day.

I guess I deserved that.

# ABOUT THE AUTHOR

Leslie Langtry is the *USA Today* bestselling author of the *Greatest Hits Mysteries* series, *Sex, Lies, & Family Vacations*, *The Hanging Tree Tales* as Max Deimos, the *Merry Wrath Mysteries*, the *Aloha Lagoon Mysteries*, and several books she hasn't finished yet, because she's very lazy.

Leslie loves puppies and cake (but she will not share her cake with puppies) and thinks praying mantids make everything better. She lives with her family and assorted animals in the Midwest, where she is currently working on her next book and trying to learn to play the ukulele.

To learn more about Leslie, visit her online at:
http://www.leslielangtry.com

Enjoyed this book? Check out these other reads available now from Leslie Langtry:

www.GemmaHallidayPublishing.com

CPSIA information can be obtained
at www.ICGtesting.com
Printed in the USA
LVHW112051180922
728694LV00004B/464